Peter Pan

A FANTASY IN FIVE ACTS

By J. M. Barrie

Acting Edition

HODDER AND STOUGHTON

CHARACTERS

(In Order of Their Appearance)

NANA (*a dog played by a boy*)
MICHAEL
MRS. DARLING
JOHN
WENDY
MR. DARLING
PETER PAN
TINKER BELL
SLIGHTLY
TOOTLES
NIBS
CURLY
FIRST TWIN
SECOND TWIN
CAPTAIN HOOK
CECCO
BILL JUKES
COOKSON
GENTLEMAN STARKEY
SKYLIGHTS
NOODLES
SMEE
TIGER LILY
PANTHER
and FAIRIES, PIRATES, INDIANS,
MERMAIDS, BIRDS, ANIMALS

SYNOPSIS OF SCENES

ACT I: *The nursery.*

ACT II: *The Never Land.*

ACT III: *The Mermaids' lagoon.*

ACT IV: *The home under the ground.*

ACT V:
    SCENE 1: *The pirate ship.*
    SCENE 2: *The nursery and the tree-tops.*

Peter Pan

ACT I

THE NURSERY: *The night nursery of the Darling family, which is the scene of our opening Act, is at the top of a rather depressed street in Bloomsbury. We have a right to place it where we will, and the reason Bloomsbury is chosen is that Mr. Roget once lived there. So did we in days when his Thesaurus was our only companion in London; and we whom he has helped to wend our way through life have always wanted to pay him a little compliment. The Darlings therefore lived in Bloomsbury.*

It is a corner house whose top window, the important one, looks upon a leafy square from which Peter used to fly up to it, to the delight of three children and no doubt the irritation of passers-by. The street is still there, though the steaming sausage shop has gone; and apparently the same cards perch now as then over the doors, inviting homeless ones to come and stay with the hospitable inhabitants. Since the days of the Darlings, however, a lick of paint has been applied; and our corner house in particular, which has swallowed its neighbour, blooms with awful freshness as if the colours had been discharged upon it through a hose. Its card now says "No children," meaning maybe that the goings-on of Wendy and her brothers have given the house a bad name. As for ourselves, we have not been in it since we went back to reclaim our old Thesaurus.

That is what we call the Darling house, but you may dump it down anywhere you like, and if you think it was your house you are very probably right. It wanders about London looking for anybody in need of it, like the little house in the Never Land.

5

The blind (which is what Peter would have called the theatre curtain if he had ever seen one) rises on that top room, a shabby little room if Mrs. Darling had not made it the hub of creation by her certainty that such it was, and adorned it to match with a loving heart and all the scrapings of her purse. The door on the right leads into the day nursery, which she has no right to have, but she made it herself with nails in her mouth and a paste-pot in her hand. This is the door the children will come in by. There are three beds and (rather oddly) a large dog-kennel; two of these beds, with the kennel, being on the left and the other on the right. The coverlets of the beds (if visitors are expected) are made out of Mrs. Darling's wedding-gown, which was such a grand affair that it still keeps them pinched. Over each bed is a china house, the size of a linnet's nest, containing a night-light. The fire, which is on our right, is burning as discreetly as if it were in custody, which in a sense it is, for supporting the mantelshelf are two wooden soldiers, home-made, begun by Mr. Darling, finished by Mrs. Darling, repainted (unfortunately) by John Darling. On the fire-guard hang incomplete parts of children's night attire. The door the parents will come in by is on the left. At the back is the bathroom door, with a cuckoo clock over it; and in the centre is the window, which is at present ever so staid and respectable, but half an hour hence (namely at 6.30 p.m.) will be able to tell a very strange tale to the police.

The only occupant of the room at present is NANA *the nurse, reclining, not as you might expect on the one soft chair, but on the floor. She is a Newfoundland dog, and though this may shock the grandiose, the not exactly affluent will make allowances. The Darlings could not afford to have a nurse, they could not afford indeed to have children; and now you are beginning to understand how they did it. Of course* NANA *has been trained by* MRS. DARLING, *but like all treasures she was born to it. In this play we shall see her chiefly inside the house, but she was just as exemplary outside, escorting the two elders to school with an umbrella in her mouth, for instance, and butting them back into line if they strayed.*

The CUCKOO CLOCK strikes six, and NANA springs into life. This first moment in the play is tremendously important, for if the actor playing NANA does not spring properly we are undone. She will probably be played by a boy, if one clever enough can be found, and must never be on two legs except on those rare occasions when an ordinary nurse would be on four. This NANA must go about all her duties in a most ordinary manner, so that you know in your bones that she performs them just so every evening at six; naturalness must be her passion; indeed, it should be the aim of every one in the play, for which she is now setting the pace. All the characters, whether grown-ups, or babies, must wear child's outlook on life as their only important adornment. If they cannot help being funny they are begged to go away. A good motto for all would be "The little less, and how much it is."

NANA, making much use of her mouth, "turns down" the beds, and carries the various articles on the fire-guard across to them. Then pushing the bathroom door open, she is seen at work on the taps preparing MICHAEL'S bath; after which she enters from the day nursery with the youngest of the family on her back.

MICHAEL. (*Obstreperous.*) I won't go to bed, I won't, I won't. Nana, it isn't six o'clock yet. Two minutes more, please, one minute more? Nana, I won't be bathed, I tell you I will not be bathed.

(*Here the bathroom door closes on them, and MRS. DAR-LING, who has perhaps heard his cry, enters the nursery. She is the loveliest lady in Bloomsbury, with a sweet mocking mouth, and as she is going out to dinner tonight she is already wearing her evening gown because she knows her children like to see her in it. It is a delicious confection made by herself out of nothing and other people's mistakes. She does not often go out to dinner, preferring when the children are in bed to sit beside them tidying up their minds, just as if they were drawers. If* WENDY *and the boys could keep awake they might see her repacking into their proper places the many articles of the mind that have strayed during the day, lingering humorously over some of their contents, wondering where on earth they picked this thing up, making discoveries sweet and not so sweet, pressing this to her cheek and hurriedly stowing that out of sight. When they wake in the morning the naughtinesses with which they went to bed are not, alas, blown away, but they are placed at the bottom of the drawer; and on the top, beautifully aired, are their prettier thoughts ready for the new day. As she enters the room she is startled to see a strange little face outside the window and a hand groping as if it wanted to come in.)*

MRS. DARLING. Who are you? (*The unknown disappears; she hurries to the window.*) No one there. And yet I feel sure I saw a face. My children! (*She throws open the bathroom door and* MICHAEL'S *head appears gaily over the bath. He splashes; she throws kisses to him and closes the door.* "WENDY, JOHN," *she cries, and gets reassuring answers from the day nursery. She sits down, relieved, on* WENDY'S *bed; and* WENDY *and* JOHN *come in, looking their smallest size, as children tend to do to a mother suddenly in fear for them.*)

JOHN. (*Histrionically.*) We are doing an act; we are playing at being you and father. (*He imitates the only father who has come under his special notice.*) A little less noise there.

WENDY. Now let us pretend we have a baby.

JOHN. (*Good-naturedly.*) I am happy to inform you, Mrs. Darling, that you are now a mother. (WENDY *gives way to ecstasy.*) You have missed the chief thing; you haven't asked, "boy or girl?"

WENDY. I am so glad to have one at all, I don't care which it is.

JOHN. (*Crushingly.*) That is just the difference between gentlemen and ladies. Now you tell me.

WENDY. I am happy to acquaint you, Mr. Darling, you are now a father.

JOHN. Boy or girl?

WENDY. (*Presenting herself.*) Girl.

JOHN. Tuts.

WENDY. You horrid.

JOHN. Go on.

WENDY. I am happy to acquaint you, Mr. Darling, you are again a father.

JOHN. Boy or girl?

WENDY. Boy. (JOHN *beams.*) Mummy, it's hateful of him.

(MICHAEL *emerges from the bathroom in* JOHN'S *old pyjamas and giving his face a last wipe with the towel.*)

MICHAEL. (*Expanding.*) Now, John, have me.

JOHN. We don't want any more.

MICHAEL. (*Contracting.*) Am I not to be born at all?

JOHN. Two is enough.

MICHAEL. (*Wheedling.*) Come, John; boy, John. (*Appalled.*) Nobody wants me!

MRS. DARLING. I do.

MICHAEL. (*With a glimmer of hope.*) Boy or girl?

MRS. DARLING. (*With one of those happy thoughts of hers.*) Boy.

(*Triumph of* MICHAEL; *discomfiture of* JOHN. MR. DARLING *arrives, in no mood unfortunately to gloat over this domestic scene. He is really a good man as bread-winners go, and it is hard luck for him to be propelled into the room now, when if we had brought him in a few minutes earlier or later he might have made a fairer impression. In the city where he sits on a stool all day, as fixed as a postage stamp, he is so like all the others on stools that you recognize him not by his face but by his stool, but at home the way to gratify him is to say that he has a distinct personality. He is very conscientious, and in the days when* MRS. DARLING *gave up keeping the house books correctly and drew pictures instead (which he called her guesses), he did all the totting up for her, holding her hand while he calculated whether they could have* WENDY *or not, and coming down on the right side. It is with regret, therefore, that we introduce him as a tornado, rushing into the nursery in evening dress, but without his coat, and brandishing in his hand a recalcitrant white tie.)*

MR. DARLING. (*Implying that he has searched for her everywhere and that the nursery is a strange place in which to find her.*) Oh, here you are, Mary.

MRS. DARLING. (*Knowing at once what is the matter.*) What is the matter, George dear?

MR. DARLING. (*As if the word were monstrous.*) Matter! This tie, it will not tie. (*He waxes sarcastic.*) Not round my neck. Round the bed-post, oh yes; twenty times have I made it up round the bed-post, but round my neck, oh dear no; begs to be excused.

MICHAEL. (*In a joyous transport.*) Say it again, father, say it again!

MR. DARLING. (*Witheringly.*) Thank you. (*Goaded by a suspiciously crooked smile on* MRS. DARLING'S *face.*) I warn you, Mary, that unless this tie is round my neck we don't go out to dinner tonight, and if I don't go out to dinner tonight I never go to the office again, and if I don't go to the office again you and I starve, and our children will be thrown into the streets.

(*The* CHILDREN *blanch as they grasp the gravity of the situation.*)

MRS. DARLING. Let me try, dear.

(*In a terrible silence their progeny cluster round them. Will she succeed? Their fate depends on it. She fails —no, she succeeds. In another moment they are wildly gay, romping round the room on each other's shoulders.* FATHER *is even a better horse than* MOTHER. MICHAEL *is dropped upon his bed,* WENDY *retires to prepare for hers,* JOHN *runs from* NANA, *who has reappeared with the bath towel.*)

JOHN. (*Rebellious.*) I won't be bathed. You needn't think it.

MR. DARLING. (*In the grand manner.*) Go and be bathed at once, sir.

(*With bent head* JOHN *follows* NANA *into the bathroom.* MR. DARLING *swells.*)

MICHAEL. (*As he is put between the sheets.*) Mother, how did you get to know me?

MR. DARLING. A little less noise there.

MICHAEL. (*Growing solemn.*) At what time was I born, mother?

MRS. DARLING. At two o'clock in the night-time, dearest.

MICHAEL. Oh mother, I hope I didn't wake you.

MRS. DARLING. They are rather sweet, don't you think, George?

MR. DARLING. (*Doting.*) There is not their equal on earth, and they are ours, ours!

(*Unfortunately* NANA *has come from the bathroom for a sponge and she collides with his trousers, the first pair he has ever had with braid on them.*)

MR. DARLING. Mary, it is too bad; just look at this; covered with hairs. Clumsy, clumsy!

(NANA *goes, a drooping figure.*)

MRS. DARLING. Let me brush you dear.

(*Once more she is successful. They are now by the fire, and* MICHAEL *is in bed doing idiotic things with a teddy bear.*)

MR. DARLING. (*Depressed.*) I sometimes think, Mary, that it is a mistake to have a dog for a nurse.

MRS. DARLING. George, Nana is a treasure.

MR. DARLING. No doubt; but I have an uneasy feeling at times that she looks upon the children as puppies.

MRS. DARLING. (*Rather faintly.*) Oh no, dear one, I am sure she knows they have souls.

MR. DARLING. (*Profoundly.*) I wonder, I wonder.

(*The opportunity has come for her to tell him of something that is on her mind.*)

MRS. DARLING. George, we must keep Nana. I will tell you why. (*Her seriousness impresses him.*) My dear, when I came into this room tonight I saw a face at the window.

MR. DARLING. (*Incredulous.*) A face at the window, three floors up? Pooh!

MRS. DARLING. It was the face of a little boy; he was trying to get in. George, this is not the first time I have seen that boy.

MR. DARLING. (*Beginning to think that this may be a man's job.*) Oho!

MRS. DARLING. (*Making sure that* MICHAEL *does not hear.*) The first time was a week ago. It was Nana's night out, and I had been drowsing here by the fire when suddenly I felt a draught, as if the window were open. I looked round and I saw that boy—in the room.

MR. DARLING. In the room?

MRS. DARLING. I screamed. Just then Nana came back and she at once sprang at him. The boy leapt for the window. She pulled down the sash quickly, but was too late to catch him.

MR. DARLING. (*Who knows he would not have been too late.*) I thought so!

MRS. DARLING. Wait. The boy escaped, but his shadow had not time to get out; down came the window and cut it clean off.

MR. DARLING. (*Heavily.*) Mary, Mary, why didn't you keep that shadow?

MRS. DARLING. (*Scoring.*) I did. I rolled it up, George; and here it is.

(*She produces it from a drawer. They unroll and examine the flimsy thing, which is not more material than a puff of smoke, and if let go would probably float into the ceiling without discolouring it. Yet it has human shape. As they nod their heads over it they present the most satisfying picture on earth, two happy parents conspiring cosily by the fire for the good of their children.*)

MR. DARLING. It is nobody I know, but he does look a scoundrel.

MRS. DARLING. I think he comes back to get his shadow, George.

MR. DARLING. (*Meaning that the miscreant has now a father to deal with.*) I dare say. (*He sees himself telling the story to the other stools at the office.*) There is money in this, my love. I shall take it to the British Museum tomorrow and have it priced.

(*The shadow is rolled up and replaced in the drawer.*)

MRS. DARLING. (*Like a guilty person.*) George, I have not told you all; I am afraid to.

MR. DARLING. (*Who knows exactly the right moment to treat a woman as a beloved child.*) Cowardy, cowardy custard.

MRS. DARLING. (*Pouting.*) No, I'm not.

MR. DARLING. Oh yes, you are.

MRS. DARLING. George, I'm not.

MR. DARLING. Then why not tell? (*Thus cleverly soothed she goes on.*)

MRS. DARLING. The boy was not alone that first time. He was accompanied by—I don't know how to describe it; by a ball of light, not as big as my fist, but it darted about the room like a living thing.

MR. DARLING. (*Though open-minded.*) That is very unusual. It escaped with the boy?

MRS. DARLING. Yes. (*Sliding her hand into his.*) George, what can all this mean?

MR. DARLING. (*Ever ready.*) What indeed!

(*This intimate scene is broken by the return of* NANA *with a bottle in her mouth.*)

MRS. DARLING. (*At once dissembling.*) What is that, Nana? Ah, of course; Michael, it is your medicine.

MICHAEL. (*Promptly.*) Won't take it.

MR. DARLING. (*Recalling his youth.*) Be a man, Michael.

MICHAEL. Won't.

MRS. DARLING. (*Weakly.*) I'll get you a lovely chocky to take after it. (*She leaves the room, though her* HUS-BAND *calls after her.*)

MR. DARLING. Mary, don't pamper him. When I was your age, Michael, I took medicine without a murmur. I said "Thank you, kind parents, for giving me bottles to make me well."

(WENDY, *who has appeared in her nightgown, hears this and believes.*)

WENDY. That medicine you sometimes take is much nastier, isn't it, father?

MR. DARLING. (*Valuing her support.*) Ever so much nastier. And as an example to you, Michael, I would take it now (*Thankfully.*) if I hadn't lost the bottle.

WENDY. (*Always glad to be of service.*) I know where it is, father. I'll fetch it.

(*She is gone before he can stop her. He turns for help to*

JOHN, *who has come from the bathroom attired for bed*.)

MR. DARLING. John, it is the most beastly stuff. It is that sticky sweet kind.

JOHN. (*Who is perhaps still playing at parents*.) Never mind, father, it will soon be over.

(*A spasm of ill-will to* JOHN *cuts through* MR. DARLING, *and is gone.* WENDY *returns panting*.)

WENDY. Here it is, father; I have been as quick as I could.

MR. DARLING. (*With a sarcasm that is completely thrown away on her*.) You have been wonderfully quick, precious quick!

(*He is now at the foot of* MICHAEL'S *bed*, NANA *is by its side, holding the medicine spoon insinuatingly in her mouth*.)

WENDY. (*Proudly, as she pours out* MR. DARLING'S *medicine*.) Michael, now you will see how father takes it.

MR. DARLING. (*Hedging*.) Michael first.

MICHAEL. (*Full of unworthy suspicions*.) Father first.

MR. DARLING. It will make me sick, you know.

JOHN. (*Lightly*.) Come on, father.

MR. DARLING. Hold your tongue, sir.

WENDY. (*Disturbed*.) I thought you took it quite easily, father, saying "Thank you kind parents, for—"

MR. DARLING. That is not the point; the point is that there is more in my glass than in Michael's spoon. It isn't fair, I swear though it were with my last breath, it is not fair.

MICHAEL. (*Coldly*.) Father, I'm waiting.

MR. DARLING. It's all very well to say you are waiting; so am I waiting.

MICHAEL. Father's a cowardy custard.

MR. DARLING. So are you a cowardy custard.

(*They are now glaring at each other.*)

MICHAEL. I am not frightened.
MR. DARLING. Neither am I frightened.
MICHAEL. Well, then, take it.
MR. DARLING. Well, then, you take it.
WENDY. (*Butting in again.*) Why not take it at the same time?
MR. DARLING. (*Haughtily.*) Certainly. Are you ready, Michael?
WENDY. (*As nothing has happened.*) One—two—three.

(MICHAEL *partakes, but* MR. DARLING *resorts to hanky-panky.*)

JOHN. Father hasn't taken his!

(MICHAEL *howls.*)

WENDY. (*Inexpressibly pained.*) Oh father!
MR. DARLING. (*Who has been hiding the glass behind him.*) What do you mean by "oh father?" Stop that row, Michael. I meant to take mine but I—missed it. (NANA *shakes her head sadly over him, and goes into the bathroom. They are all looking as if they did not admire him, and nothing so dashes a temperamental man.*) I say, I have just thought of a splendid joke. (*They brighten.*) I shall pour my medicine into Nana's bowl, and she will drink it thinking it is milk! (*The pleasantry does not appeal, but he prepares the joke, listening for appreciation.*)
WENDY. Poor darling Nana!
MR. DARLING. You silly little things; to your beds every one of you; I am ashamed of you.

They steal to their beds as MRS. DARLING *returns with the chocolate.*)

MRS. DARLING. Well, it is all over?

MICHAEL. Father didn't— (FATHER *glares*.)

MR. DARLING. All over, dear, quite satisfactorily. (NANA *comes back*.) Nana, good dog, good girl; I have put a little milk into your bowl. (*The bowl is by the kennel, and* NANA *begins to lap, only begins. She retreats into the kennel*.)

MRS. DARLING. What is the matter, Nana?

MR. DARLING. (*Uneasily*.) Nothing, nothing.

MRS. DARLING. (*Smelling the bowl*.) George, it is your medicine!

(*The* CHILDREN *break into lamentation. He gives his* WIFE *an imploring look; he is begging for one smile, but does not get it. In consequence he goes from bad to worse*.)

MR. DARLING. It was only a joke. Much good my wearing myself to the bone trying to be funny in this house.

WENDY. (*On her knees by the kennel*.) Father, Nana is crying.

MR. DARLING. Coddle her; nobody coddles me. Oh dear no. I am only the bread-winner, why should I be coddled? Why, why, why?

MRS. DARLING. George, not so loud; the servants will hear you.

(*There is only one maid, absurdly small too, but they have got into the way of calling her the servants*.)

MR. DARLING. (*Defiant*.) Let them hear me; bring in the whole world. (*The desperate man, who has not been in fresh air for days, has now lost all self-control*.) I refuse to allow that dog to lord it in my nursery for one hour longer. (NANA *supplicates him*.) In vain, in vain, the proper place for you is the yard, and there you go to be tied up this instant.

(NANA *again retreats into the kennel, and the* CHILDREN *add their prayers to hers*.)

B

MRS. DARLING. (*Who knows how contrite he will be for this presently.*) George, George, remember what I told you about that boy.

MR. DARLING. Am I master in this house or is she? (*To* NANA *fiercely.*) Come along. (*He thrusts at her, but she indicates that she has reasons not worth troubling him with for remaining where she is. He resorts to a false bonhomie.*) There, there, did she think he was angry with her, poor Nana? (*She wriggles a response in the affirmative.*) Good Nana, pretty Nana. (*She has seldom been called pretty, and it has the old effect. She plays rub-a-dub with her paws, which is how a dog blushes.*) She will come to her kind master, won't she? won't she? (*She advances, retreats, waggles her head, her tail, and eventually goes to him. He seizes her collar in an iron grip and amid the cries of his progeny drags her from the room. They listen, for her remonstrances are not inaudible.*)

MRS. DARLING. Be brave, my dears.

WENDY. He is chaining Nana up!

(*This unfortunately is what he is doing, though we cannot see him. Let us hope that he then retires to his study, looks up the word "temper" in his Thesaurus, and under the influence of those benign pages becomes a better man. In the meantime the* CHILDREN *have been put to bed in unwonted silence, and* MRS. DARLING *lights the NIGHT-LIGHTS over the beds.*)

JOHN. (*As the BARKING below goes on.*) She is awfully unhappy.

WENDY. That is not Nana's unhappy bark. That is her bark when she smells danger.

MRS. DARLING. (*Remembering that boy.*) Danger! Are you sure, Wendy?

WENDY. (*The one of the family, for there is one in every family, who can be trusted to know or not to know.*) Oh yes.

(*Her* MOTHER *looks this way and that from the window.*)

JOHN. Is anything there?

MRS. DARLING. All quite quiet and still. Oh, how I wish I was not going out to dinner tonight.

MICHAEL. Can anything harm us, mother, after the night-lights are lit?

MRS. DARLING. Nothing, precious. They are the eyes a mother leaves behind her to guard her children.

(*Nevertheless we may be sure she means to tell* LIZA, *the little maid, to look in on them frequently till she comes home. She goes from bed to bed, after her custom, tucking them in and crooning a lullaby.*)

MICHAEL. (*Drowsily.*) Mother, I'm glad of you.

MRS. DARLING. (*With a last look round, her hand on the switch.*) Dear night-lights that protect my sleeping babes, burn clear and steadfast tonight.

(*The nursery* DARKENS *and she is gone, intentionally leaving the door ajar. Something uncanny is going to happen, we expect, for a quiver has passed through the room, just sufficient to touch the* NIGHT-LIGHTS. *They blink three times one after the other and go out, precisely as* CHILDREN (*whom familiarity has made them resemble*) *fall asleep. There is another* LIGHT *in the room now, no larger than* MRS. DAR-LING'S *fist, and in the time we have taken to say this it has been into the drawers and wardrobe and searched pockets, as it darts about looking for a certain shadow. Then the window is blown open, probably by the smallest and therefore most mischievous star, and* PETER PAN *flies into the room. In so far as he is dressed at all it is in autumn leaves and cobwebs.*)

PETER. (*In a whisper.*) Tinker Bell, Tink, are you there? (*A* JUG *lights up.*) Oh, do come out of that jug. (TINK *flashes hither and thither.*) Do you know where they put it? (*The answer comes as of a tingle of* BELLS; *it is the*

fairy language. PETER *can speak it, but it bores him.*)
Which big box? This one? But which drawer? Yes, do
show me. (TINK *pops into the drawer where the shadow
is, but before* PETER *can reach it,* WENDY *moves in her
sleep. He flies onto the mantelshelf as a hiding-place.
Then, as she has not waked, he flutters over the beds as
an easy way to observe the occupants, closes the window
softly, wafts himself to the drawer and scatters its contents to the floor, as kings on their wedding day toss ha'-
pence to the crowd. In his joy at finding his shadow he
forgets that he has shut up* TINK *in the drawer. He sits
on the floor with the shadow, confident that he and it
will join like drops of water. Then he tries to stick it on
with soap from the bathroom, and this failing also, he
subsides dejectedly on the floor. This wakens* WENDY, *who
sits up, and is pleasantly interested to see a stranger.*)

WENDY. (*Courteously.*) Boy, why are you crying?

(*He jumps up, and crossing to the foot of the bed bows to
her in the fairy way.* WENDY, *impressed, bows to
him from the bed.*)

PETER. What is your name?
WENDY. (*Well satisfied.*) Wendy Moira Angela Dar-
ling. What is yours?
PETER. (*Finding it lamentably brief.*) Peter Pan.
WENDY. Is that all?
PETER. (*Biting his lip.*) Yes.
WENDY. (*Politely.*) I am so sorry.
PETER. It doesn't matter.
WENDY. Where do you live?
PETER. Second to the right and then straight on till
morning.
WENDY. What a funny address!
PETER. No, it isn't.
WENDY. I mean, is that what they put on the letters?
PETER. Don't get any letters.
WENDY. But your mother gets letters?
PETER. Don't have a mother.

WENDY. Peter!

(*She leaps out of bed to put her arms round him, but he draws back; he does not know why, but he knows he must draw back.*)

PETER. You mustn't touch me.
WENDY. Why?
PETER. No one must ever touch me.
WENDY. Why?
PETER. I don't know.

(*He is never touched by anyone in the play.*)

WENDY. No wonder you were crying.
PETER. I wasn't crying. But I can't get my shadow to stick on.
WENDY. It has come off! How awful. (*Looking at the spot where he had lain.*) Peter, you have been trying to stick it on with soap!
PETER. (*Snappily.*) Well then?
WENDY. It must be sewn on.
PETER. What is "sewn"?
WENDY. You are dreadfully ignorant.
PETER. No, I'm not.
WENDY. I will sew it on for you, my little man. But we must have more light. (*She touches something, and to his astonishment the room is ILLUMINATED.*) Sit here. I dare say it will hurt a little.
PETER. (*A recent remark of hers rankling.*) I never cry. (*She seems to attach the shadow. He tests the combination.*) It isn't quite itself yet.
WENDY. Perhaps I should have ironed it. (*It awakes and is as glad to be back with him as he to have it. He and his shadow dance together. He is showing off now. He crows like a cock. He would fly in order to impress* WENDY *further if he knew that there is anything unusual in that.*)
PETER. Wendy, look, look; oh the cleverness of me!

WENDY. You conceit; of course I did nothing!

PETER. You did a little.

WENDY. (*Wounded.*) A little! If I am no use I can at least withdraw.

(*With one haughty leap she is again in bed with the sheet over her face. Popping on to the end of the bed the artful one appeals.*)

PETER. Wendy, don't withdraw. I can't help crowing, Wendy, when I'm pleased with myself. Wendy, one girl is worth more than twenty boys.

WENDY. (*Peeping over the sheet.*) You really think so, Peter?

PETER. Yes, I do.

WENDY. I think it's perfectly sweet of you, and I shall get up again. (*They sit together on the side of the bed.*) I shall give you a kiss if you like.

PETER. Thank you. (*He holds out his hand.*)

WENDY. (*Aghast.*) Don't you know what a kiss is?

PETER. I shall know when you give it me. (*Not to hurt his feelings she gives him her thimble.*) Now shall I give you a kiss?

WENDY. (*Primly.*) If you please. (*He pulls an acorn button off his person and bestows it on her. She is shocked but considerate.*) I will wear it on this chain round my neck. Peter, how old are you?

PETER. (*Blithely.*) I don't know, but quite young, Wendy. I ran away the day I was born.

WENDY. Ran away, why?

PETER. Because I heard father and mother talking of what I was to be when I became a man. I want always to be a little boy and to have fun; so I ran away to Kensington Gardens and lived a long time among the fairies.

WENDY. (*With great eyes.*) You know fairies, Peter!

PETER. (*Surprised that this should be a recommendation.*) Yes, but they are nearly all dead now. (*Baldly.*) You see, Wendy, when the first baby laughed for the first time, the laugh broke into a thousand pieces and they all went skipping about, and that was the beginning of fairies. And now when every new baby is born its first laugh becomes a fairy. So there ought to be one fairy for every boy or girl.

WENDY. (*Breathlessly.*) Ought to be? Isn't there?

PETER. Oh no. Children know such a lot now. Soon they don't believe in fairies, and every time a child says "I don't believe in fairies" there is a fairy somewhere that falls down dead. (*He skips about heartlessly.*)

WENDY. Poor things!

PETER. (*To whom this statement recalls a forgotten friend.*) I can't think where she has gone. Tinker Bell, Tink, where are you?

WENDY. (*Thrilling.*) Peter, you don't mean to tell me that there is a fairy in this room!

PETER. (*Flitting about in search.*) She came with me. You don't hear anything, do you?

WENDY. I hear—the only sound I hear is like a tinkle of bells.

PETER. That is the fairy language. I hear it too.

WENDY. It seems to come from over there.

PETER. (*With shameless glee.*) Wendy, I believe I shut her up in that drawer!

(*He releases* TINK, *who darts about in a fury using language it is perhaps as well we don't understand.*)

You needn't say that; I'm very sorry, but how could I know you were in the drawer?

WENDY. (*Her eyes dancing in pursuit of the delicious creature.*) Oh, Peter, if only she would stand still and let me see her!

PETER. (*Indifferently.*) They hardly ever stand still.

(*To show that she can do even this* TINK *pauses between two ticks of the cuckoo clock.*)

WENDY. I see her, the lovely! where is she now?

PETER. She is behind the clock. Tink, this lady wishes you were her fairy. (*The answer comes immediately.*)

WENDY. What does she say?

PETER. She is not very polite. She says you are a great ugly girl, and that she is my fairy. You know, Tink, you can't be my fairy because I am a gentleman and you are a lady.

(TINK *replies*.)

WENDY. What did she say?

PETER. She said "You silly ass." She is quite a common girl, you know. She is called Tinker Bell because she mends the fairy pots and kettles.

(*They have reached a chair*, WENDY *in the ordinary way and* PETER *through a hole in the back*.)

WENDY. Where do you live now?

PETER. With the lost boys.

WENDY. Who are they?

PETER. They are the children who fall out of their prams when the nurse is looking the other way. If they are not claimed in seven days they are sent far away to the Never Land. I'm captain.

WENDY. What fun it must be.

PETER. (*Craftily*.) Yes, but we are rather lonely. You see, Wendy, we have no female companionship.

WENDY. Are none of the other children girls?

PETER. Oh no; girls, you know, are much too clever to fall out of their prams.

WENDY. Peter, it is perfectly lovely the way you talk about girls. John there just despises us.

(PETER, *for the first time, has a good look at* JOHN. *He then neatly tumbles him out of bed*.)

You wicked! you are not captain here. (*She bends over her* BROTHER *who is prone on the floor*.) After all he hasn't wakened, and you meant to be kind. (*Having now done her duty she forgets* JOHN, *who blissfully sleeps on*.) Peter, you may give me a kiss.

PETER. (*Cynically.*) I thought you would want it back.

(*He offers her the thimble.*)

WENDY. (*Artfully.*) Oh dear, I didn't mean a kiss, Peter. I meant a thimble.

PETER. (*Only half placated.*) What is that?

WENDY. It is like this. (*She leans forward to give a demonstration, but something prevents the meeting of their faces.*)

PETER. (*Satisfied.*) Now shall I give you a thimble?

WENDY. If you please. (*Before he can even draw near she screams.*)

PETER. What is it?

WENDY. It was exactly as if someone were pulling my hair!

PETER. That must have been Tink. I never knew her so naughty before.

(TINK *speaks. She is in the jug again.*)

WENDY. What does she say?

PETER. She says she will do that every time I give you a thimble.

WENDY. But why?

PETER. (*Equally nonplussed.*) Why, Tink? (*He has to translate the answer.*) She said "You silly ass" again.

WENDY. She is very impertinent. (*They are sitting on the floor now.*) Peter, why did you come to our nursery window?

PETER. To try to hear stories. None of us know any stories.

WENDY. How perfectly awful!

PETER. Do you know why swallows build in the eaves of houses? It is to listen to the stories. Wendy, your mother was telling you such a lovely story.

WENDY. Which story was it?

PETER. About the prince, and he couldn't find the lady who wore the glass slipper.

WENDY. That was Cinderella. Peter, he found her and they were happy ever after.

PETER. I am glad. (*They have worked their way along the floor close to each other, but he now jumps up.*)

WENDY. Where are you going?

PETER. (*Already on his way to the window.*) To tell the other boys.

WENDY. Don't go, Peter. I know lots of stories. The stories I could tell to the boys!

PETER. (*Gleaming.*) Come on! We'll fly.

WENDY. Fly? You can fly!

(*How he would like to rip those stories out of her; he is dangerous now.*)

PETER. Wendy, come with me.

WENDY. Oh dear, I mustn't. Think of mother. Besides, I can't fly.

PETER. I'll teach you.

WENDY. How lovely to fly!

PETER. I'll teach you how to jump on the wind's back and then away we go. Wendy, when you are sleeping in your silly bed you might be flying about with me, saying funny things to the stars. There are mermaids, Wendy, with long tails. (*She just succeeds in remaining on the nursery floor.*) Wendy, how we should all respect you.

(*At this she strikes her colours.*)

WENDY. Of course it's awfully fas-cin-a-ting! Would you teach John and Michael to fly too?

PETER. (*Indifferently.*) If you like.

WENDY. (*Playing rum-tum on* JOHN.) John, wake up; there is a boy here who is to teach us to fly.

JOHN. Is there? Then I shall get up. (*He raises his head from the floor.*) Hullo, I am up!

WENDY. Michael, open your eyes. This boy is to teach us to fly.

(*The sleepers are at once as awake as their father's razor;*

but before a question can be asked NANA'S *bark is heard.*)

JOHN. Out with the light, quick, hide!

(*When the maid* LIZA, *who is so small that when she says she will never see ten again one can scarcely believe her, enters with a firm hand on the troubled* NANA'S *chain the room is in comparative darkness.*)

LIZA. There, you suspicious brute, they are perfectly safe, aren't they? Every one of the little angels sound asleep in bed. Listen to their gentle breathing. (NANA'S *sense of smell here helps to her undoing instead of hindering it. She knows that they are in the room.* MICHAEL, *who is behind the window curtain, is so encouraged by* LIZA'S *last remark that he breathes too loudly.* NANA *knows that kind of breathing and tries to break from her keeper's control.*) No more of it, Nana. (*Wagging a finger at her.*) I warn you if you bark again I shall go straight for Master and Missus and bring them home from the party, and then won't Master whip you just! Come along, you naughty dog.

(*The unhappy* NANA *is led away. The* CHILDREN *emerge exulting from their various hiding-places. In their brief absence from the scene strange things have been done to them; but it is not for us to reveal a mysterious secret of the stage. They look just the same.*)

JOHN. I say, can you really fly?
PETER. Look! (*He is now over their heads.*)
WENDY. Oh, how sweet!
PETER. I'm sweet, oh, I am sweet!

(*It looks so easy that they try it first from the floor and then from their beds, without encouraging results.*)

JOHN. (*Rubbing his knees.*) How do you do it?

PETER. (*Descending.*) You just think lovely wonderful thoughts and they lift you up in the air. (*He is off again.*)

JOHN. You are so nippy at it; couldn't you do it very slowly once? (PETER *does it slowly.*) I've got it now, Wendy. (*He tries; no, he has not got it, poor stay-at-home, though he knows the names of all the counties in England and* PETER *does not know one.*)

PETER. I must blow the fairy dust on you first. (*Fortunately his garments are smeared with it and he blows some dust on each.*) Now, try; try from the bed. Just wriggle your shoulders this way, and then let go.

(*The gallant* MICHAEL *is the first to let go, and is borne across the room.*)

MICHAEL. (*With a yell that should have disturbed* LIZA.) I flewed!

(JOHN *lets go, and meets* WENDY *near the bathroom door though they had both aimed in an opposite direction.*)

WENDY. Oh, lovely!
JOHN. (*Tending to be upside down.*) How ripping!
MICHAEL. (*Playing whack on a chair.*) I do like it!
THE THREE. Look at me, look at me, look at me!

(*They are not nearly so elegant in the air as* PETER, *but their heads have bumped the ceiling, and there is nothing more delicious than that.*)

JOHN. (*Who can even go backwards.*) I say, why shouldn't we go out?
PETER. There are pirates.
JOHN. Pirates! (*He grabs his tall Sunday hat.*) Let us go at once!

(TINK *does not like it. She darts at their hair. From*

down below in the street the lighted window must present an unwonted spectacle: the shadows of children revolving in the room like a merry-go-round. This is perhaps what MR. *and* MRS. DARLING *see as they come hurrying home from the party, brought by* NANA *who, you may be sure, has broken her chain.* PETER'S *accomplice, the little star, has seen them coming, and again the WINDOW blows open.*)

PETER. (*As if he had heard the star whisper* Cave.) Now come!

(*Breaking the circle he flies out of the window over the trees of the square and over the house-tops, and the others follow like a flight of birds. The broken-hearted* FATHER *and* MOTHER *arrive just in time to get a nip from* TINK *as she too sets out for the Never Land.*)

ACT II

THE NEVER LAND: *When the blind goes up all is so dark that you scarcely know it has gone up. This is because if you were to see the island bang (as* PETER *would say) the wonders of it might hurt your eyes. If you all came in spectacles perhaps you could see it bang, but to make a rule of that kind would be a pity. The first thing seen is merely some whitish dots trudging along the sward, and you can guess from their tinkling that they are probably fairies of the commoner sort going home afoot from some party and having a cheery tiff by the way. Then* PETER'S *star wakes up, and in the blink of it, which is much stronger than in our stars, you can make out masses of trees, and you think you see wild beasts stealing past to drink, though what you see is not the beasts themselves but only the shadows of them. They are really out pictorially to greet* PETER *in the way they think he would like them to greet him; and for the same reason the mermaids basking in the lagoon beyond the trees are carefully combing their hair; and for the same reason the pirates are landing invisibly from the longboat, invisibly to you but not to the redskins, whom none can see or hear because they are on the war-path. The whole island, in short, which has been having a slack time in* PETER'S *absence, is now in a ferment because the tidings have leaked out that he is on his way back; and everybody and everything know that they will catch it from him if they don't give satisfaction. While you have been told this the sun (another of his servants) has been bestirring himself. Those of you who may have thought it wiser after all to begin this Act in spectacles may now take them off.*

What you see is the Never Land. You have often half seen it before, or even three-quarters, after the

30

*night-lights were lit, and you might then have beached
your coracle on it if you had not always at the great
moment fallen asleep. I dare say you have chucked
things on to it, the things you can't find in the morning. In the daytime you think the Never Land is
only make-believe, and so it is to the likes of you,
but this is the Never-Land come true. It is an open-
air scene, a forest, with a beautiful lagoon beyond
but not really far away, for the Never Land is very
compact, not large and sprawly with tedious distances
between one adventure and another, but nicely crammed.
It is summer time on the streets and on the lagoon
but winter on the river, which is not remarkable
on* PETER'S *island where all the four seasons may
pass while you are filling a jug at the well.* PETER'S
*home is at this very spot, but you could not point
out the way into it even if you were told which is the
entrance, not even if you were told that there are
seven of them. You know now because you have just
seen one of the lost boys emerge. The holes in these
seven great hollow trees are the "doors" down to*
PETER'S *home, and he made seven because, despite
his cleverness, he thought seven boys must need seven
doors.*

The boy who has emerged from his tree is SLIGHTLY,
*who has perhaps been driven from the abode below
by companions less musical then himself, Quite
possibly a genius,* SLIGHTLY *has with him his home-
made whistle to which he capers entrancingly, with
no audience save a Never ostrich which is also music-
ally inclined. Unable to imitate* SLIGHTLY'S *graces
the bird falls so low as to burlesque them and is
driven from the entertainment. Other* LOST BOYS
*climb up the trunks or drop from branches, and now
we see the six of them, all in the skins of animals
they think they have shot, and so round and furry in
them that if they fall they roll.* TOOTLES *is not the
least brave though the most unfortunate of this gallant
band. He has been in fewer adventures than any*

of them because the big things constantly happen while he has stepped round the corner; he will go off, for instance, in some quiet hour to gather fire-wood, and then when he returns the others will be sweeping up the blood. Instead of souring his nature this has sweetened it and he is the humblest of the band. NIBS is more gay and debonair, SLIGHTLY more conceited. SLIGHTLY thinks he remembers the days before he was lost, with their manners and customs. CURLY is a pickle, and so often has he had to deliver up his person when PETER said sternly, "Stand forth the one who did this thing," that now he stands forth whether he has done it or not. The other two are FIRST TWIN and SECOND TWIN, who cannot be described because we should probably be describing the wrong one. Hunkering on the ground or peeping out of their holes, the six are not unlike village gossips gathered round the pump.

TOOTLES. Has Peter come back yet, Slightly?

SLIGHTLY. (*With a solemnity that he thinks suits the occasion.*) No, Tootles, no.

(*They are like dogs waiting for the master to tell them that the day has begun.*)

CURLY. (*As if PETER might be listening.*) I do wish he would come back.

TOOTLES. I am always afraid of the pirates when Peter is not here to protect us.

SLIGHTLY. I am not afraid of pirates. Nothing frightens me. But I do wish Peter would come back and tell us whether he has heard anything more about Cinderella.

SECOND TWIN. (*With diffidence.*) Slightly, I dreamt last night that the prince found Cinderella.

FIRST TWIN. (*Who is intellectually the superior of the two.*) Twin, I think you should not have dreamt that, for I didn't, and Peter may say we oughtn't to dream differently, being twins, you know.

TOOTLES. I am awfully anxious about Cinderella. You see, not knowing anything about my own mother I am fond of thinking that she was rather like Cinderella.

(*This is received with derision.*)

NIBS. All I remember about my mother is that she often said to father, "Oh how I wish I had a cheque book of my own." I don't know what a cheque book is, but I should just love to give my mother one.

SLIGHTLY. (*As usual.*) My mother was fonder of me than your mothers were of you. (*Uproar.*) Oh yes, she was. Peter had to make up names for you, but my mother had wrote my name on the pinafore I was lost in. "Slightly Soiled"; that's my name.

(*They fall upon him pugnaciously; not that they are really worrying about their mothers, who are now as important to them as a piece of string, but because any excuse is good enough for a shindy. Not for long is he belaboured, for a sound is heard that sends them scurrying down their holes: in a second of time the scene is bereft of human life. What they have heard from near by is a verse of the dreadful song with which on the Never Land the* PIRATES *stealthily trumpet their approach*—

> Yo ho, you ho, the pirate life,
> The flag of skull and bones,
> A merry hour, a hempen rope,
> And hey for Davy Jones!

Cont P 35

The PIRATES *appear upon the frozen river dragging a raft, on which reclines among cushions that dark and fearful man,* CAPTAIN JAS HOOK. *A more villainous-looking brotherhood of men never hung in a row on Execution dock. Here, his great arms bare, pieces of eight in his ears as ornaments, is the handsome* CECCO, *who cut his name on the back of the governor of the prison at Goa. Heavier in the pull is the gigantic black who has had many names since*

C

the first one terrified dusky children on the banks of the Guidjo-mo. BILL JUKES *comes next, every inch of him tattooed, the same* JUKES *who got six dozen on the* Walrus *from* FLINT. *Following these are* COOKSON, *said to be* BLACK MURPHY'S *brother [but this was never proved]; and* GENTLEMAN STARKEY, *once an usher in a school; and* SKYLIGHTS *[Morgan's Skylights]; and* NOODLER, *whose hands are fixed on backwards; and the spectacled boatswain,* SMEE, *the only Nonconformist in* HOOK'S *crew; and other ruffians long known and feared on the Spanish main.*

Cruellest jewel in that dark setting is HOOK *himself, cadaverous and blackavized, his hair dressed in long curls which look like black candles about to melt, his eyes blue as the forget-me-not and of a profound insensibility, save when he claws, at which time a red spot appears in them. He has an iron hook instead of a right hand, and it is with this he claws. He is never more sinister than when he is most polite, and the elegance of his diction, the distinction of his demeanour, show him one of a different class from his crew, a solitary among uncultured companions. This courtliness impresses even his victims on the high seas, who wrote that he always says "Sorry" when prodding them along the plank. A man of indomitable courage, the only thing at which he flinches is the sight of his own blood, which is thick and of an unusual colour. At his public school they said of him that he "bled yellow". In dress he apes the dandiacal associated with Charles II, having heard it said in an earlier period of his career that he bore a strange resemblance to the ill-fated Stuarts. A holder of his own contrivance is in his mouth enabling him to smoke two cigars at once. Those, however, who have seen him in the flesh, which is an inadequate term for his earthly tenement, agree that the grimmest part of him is his iron claw.*

They continue their distasteful singing as they disembark—

Avast, belay, yo ho, heave to,
A-pirating we go,
And if we're parted by a shot
We're sure to meet below!

(NIBS, *the only one of the boys who has not sought safety in his tree, is seen for a moment near the lagoon, and* STARKEY'S *pistol is at once up-raised. The captain twists his hook in him.*)

STARKEY. (*Abject.*) Captain, let go!

HOOK. Put back that pistol, first.

STARKEY. 'Twas one of those boys you hate; I could have shot him dead.

HOOK. Ay, and the sound would have brought Tiger Lily's redskins on us. Do you want to lose your scalp?

SMEE. (*Wriggling his cutlass pleasantly.*) That is true. Shall I after him, Captain, and tickle him with Johnny Corkscrew? Johnny is a silent fellow.

HOOK. Not now. He is only one, and I want to mischief all the seven. Scatter and look for them. (*The* BOATSWAIN *whistles his instructions, and the* MEN *disperse on their frightful errand. With none to hear save* SMEE, HOOK *becomes confidential.*) Most of all I want their captain, Peter Pan. 'Twas he cut off my arm. I have waited long to shake his hand with this. (*Luxuriating.*) Oh, I'll tear him!

SMEE. (*Always ready for a chat.*) Yet I have oft heard you say your hook was worth a score of hands, for combing the hair and other homely uses.

HOOK. If I was a mother I would pray to have my children born with this instead of that. (*His left arm creeps nervously behind him. He has a galling remembrance.*) Smee, Pan flung my arm to a crocodile that happened to be passing by.

SMEE. I have often noticed your strange dread of crocodiles.

HOOK. (*Pettishly.*) Not of crocodiles but of that one crocodile. (*He lays bare a lacerated heart.*) The brute liked my arm so much, Smee, that he has followed me ever since, from sea to sea, from land to land, licking his lips for the rest of me.

SMEE. (*Looking for the bright side.*) In a way it is a sort of compliment.

HOOK. (*With dignity.*) I want no such compliments; I want Peter Pan, who first gave the brute his taste for me. Smee, that crocodile would have had me before now, but by a lucky chance he swallowed a clock, and it goes tick, tick, tick, tick inside him; and so before he can reach me I hear the tick and bolt. (*He emits a hollow rumble.*) Once I heard it strike six within him.

SMEE. (*Sombrely.*) Some day the clock will run down, and then he'll get you.

HOOK. (*A broken man.*) Ay, that is the fear that haunts me. (*He rises.*) Smee, this seat is hot; odds, bobs, hammer and tongs, I am burning.

(*He has been sitting, he thinks, on one of the island mush-rooms, which are of enormous size. But this is a hand-painted one placed here in times of danger to conceal a chimney. They remove it, and tell-tale smoke issues; also, alas, the sound of children's voices.*)

SMEE. A chimney!

HOOK. (*Avidly.*) Listen! Smee, 'tis plain they live here, beneath the ground. (*He replaces the mushroom. His brain works tortuously.*)

SMEE. (*Hopefully.*) Unrip your plan, Captain.

HOOK. To return to the boat and cook a large rich cake of jolly thickness with sugar on it, green sugar. There can be but one room below, for there is but one chimney. The silly moles had not the sense to see that they did not need a door apiece. We must leave the cake on the shore of the mermaids' lagoon. These boys are always swimming about there, trying to catch the mermaids. They will find the cake and gobble it up, because, having no mother, they don't know how dangerous 'tis to eat rich damp cake. They will die!

SMEE. (*Fascinated.*) It is the wickedest, prettiest policy ever I heard of.

HOOK. (*Meaning well.*) Shake hands on 't.

SMEE. No, Captain, no.

(*He has to link with the hook, but he does not join in the song.*)

HOOK. Yo ho, yo ho, when I say "paw,"
   By fear they're overtook,
   Naught's left upon your bones when you
   Have shaken hands with Hook!

(*Frightened by a tug at his hand, SMEE is joining in the chorus when another sound stills them both. It is a tick, tick, as of a clock, whose significance HOOK is, naturally, the first to recognize. "The crocodile!" he cries, and totters from the scene. SMEE follows. A huge CROCODILE, of one thought compact, passes across ticking, and oozes after them. The wood is now so silent that you may be sure it is full of red-skins. TIGER LILY comes first. She is the belle of the Piccaninny tribe, whose braves would all have her to wife, but she wards them off with a hatchet. She puts her ear to the ground and listens, then beckons, and GREAT BIG LITTLE PANTHER and the tribe are around her, carpeting the ground. Far away someone treads on a dry leaf.*)

TIGER LILY. Pirates! (*They do not draw their knives; the knives slip into their hands.*) Have um scalps? What you say?

PANTHER. Scalp um, oho, velly quick.

THE BRAVES. (*In corroboration.*) Ugh, ugh, wah.

(*A FIRE is lit and they dance round and over it till they seem part of the leaping flames. TIGER LILY invokes Manitou; the pipe of peace is broken; and they crawl off like a long snake that has not fed for many moons.*

TOOTLES *peers after the tail and summons the other*
BOYS, *who issue from their holes.*)

TOOTLES. They are gone.

SLIGHTLY. (*Almost losing confidence in himself.*) I do
wish Peter was here.

FIRST TWIN. H'sh! What is that? (*He is gazing at the
lagoon and shrinks back.*) It is wolves, and they are
chasing Nibs!

(*The baying* WOLVES *are upon them quicker than any
boy can scuttle down his tree.*)

NIBS. (*Falling among his comrades.*) Save me, save me!

TOOTLES. What should we do?

SECOND TWIN. What would Peter do?

SLIGHTLY. Peter would look at them through his legs;
let us do what Peter would do.

(*The* BOYS *advance backwards, looking between their
legs at the snarling red-eyed* ENEMY, *who trot away
foiled.*)

FIRST TWIN. (*Swaggering.*) We have saved you, Nibs.
Did you see the pirates?

NIBS. (*Sitting up, and agreeably aware that the centre
of interest is now about to pass to him.*) No, but I saw a won-
derfuller thing, Twin. (*All mouths open for the informa-
tion to be dropped into them.*) High over the lagoon I saw
the loveliest great white bird. It is flying this way. (*They
search the firmament.*)

TOOTLES. What kind of a bird, do you think?

NIBS. (*Awed.*) I don't know; but it looked so weary,
and as it flies it moans "Poor Wendy".

SLIGHTLY. (*Instantly.*) I remember now there are birds
called Wendies.

FIRST TWIN. (*Who has flown to a high branch.*) See,
it comes, the Wendy! (*They all see it now.*) How white
it is! (*A dot of light is pursuing the bird malignantly.*)

TOOTLES. That is Tinker Bell. Tink is trying to hurt the Wendy. (*He makes a cup of his hands and calls.*) Hullo, Tink! (*A response comes down in the fairy language.*) She says Peter wants us to shoot the Wendy.

NIBS. Let us do what Peter wishes.

SLIGHTLY. Ay, shoot it; quick, bows and arrows.

TOOTLES. (*First with his bow.*) Out of the way, Tink; I'll shoot it. (*His bolt goes home. and* WENDY, *who has been fluttering among the treetops in her white nightgown, falls straight to earth. No one could be more proud than* TOOTLES.) I have shot the Wendy; Peter will be so pleased. (*From some tree on which* TINK *is roosting comes the tinkle we can now translate, "You silly ass."* TOOTLES *falters.*) Why do you say that? (*The* OTHERS *feel that he may have blundered, and draw away from* TOOTLES.)

SLIGHTLY. (*Examining the fallen one more minutely.*) This is no bird; I think it must be a lady.

NIBS. (*Who would have preferred it to be a bird.*) And Tootles has killed her.

CURLY. Now I see, Peter was bringing her to us. (*They wonder for what object.*)

SECOND TWIN. To take care of us? (*Undoubtedly for some diverting purpose.*)

OMNES. (*Though every one of them had wanted to have a shot at her.*) Oh, Tootles!

TOOTLES. (*Gulping.*) I did it. When ladies used to come to me in dreams I said "Pretty mother," but when she really came I shot her! (*He perceives the necessity of a solitary life for him.*) Friends, good-bye.

SEVERAL. (*Not very enthusiastic.*) Don't go.

TOOTLES. I must; I am so afraid of Peter.

(*He has gone but a step toward oblivion when he is stopped by a crowing as of some victorious cock.*)

OMNES. Peter!

(*They make a paling of themselves in front of* WENDY *as* PETER *skims round the treetops and reaches earth.*)

PETER. Greeting, boys! (*Their silence chafes him.*) I am back; why do you not cheer? Great news, boys, I have brought at last a mother for us all.

SLIGHTLY. (*Vaguely.*) Ay, ay.

PETER. She flew this way; have you not seen her?

SECOND TWIN. (*As* PETER *evidently thinks her important.*) Oh mournful day!

TOOTLES. (*Making a break in the paling.*) Peter, I will show her to you.

THE OTHERS. (*Closing the gap.*) No, no.

TOOTLES. (*Majestically.*) Stand back all, and let Peter see.

(*The paling dissolves, and* PETER *sees* WENDY *prone on the ground.*)

PETER. Wendy, with an arrow in her heart? (*He plucks it out.*) Wendy is dead. (*He is not so much pained as puzzled.*)

CURLY. I thought it was only flowers that die

PETER. Perhaps she is frightened at being dead? (*None of them can say as to that.*) Whose arrow? (*Not one of them looks at* TOOTLES.)

TOOTLES. Mine, Peter.

PETER. (*Raising it as a dagger.*) Oh dastard hand!

TOOTLES. (*Kneeling and baring his breast.*) Strike, Peter; strike true.

PETER. (*Undergoing a singular experience.*) I cannot strike; there is something stays my hand.

(*In fact* WENDY'S *arm has risen.*)

NIBS. 'Tis she, the Wendy lady. See, her arm. (*To help a friend.*) I think she said "Poor Tootles."

PETER. (*Investigating.*) She lives!

SLIGHTLY. (*Authoritatively.*) The Wendy lady lives.

(*The delightful feeling that they have been cleverer than they thought comes over them and they applaud themselves.*)

PETER. (*Holding up a button that is attached to her chain.*) See, the arrow struck against this, It is a kiss I gave her; it has saved her life.

SLIGHTLY. I remember kisses; let me see it. (*He takes it in his hand.*) Ay, that is a kiss.

PETER. Wendy, get better quickly and I'll take you to see the mermaids. She is awfully anxious to see a mermaid.

(TINKER BELL, *who may have been off visiting her relations, returns to the wood and, under the impression that* WENDY *has been got rid of, is whistling as gaily as a canary. She is not wholly heartless, but is so small that she has only room for one feeling at a time.*)

CURLY. Listen to Tink rejoicing because she thinks the Wendy is dead! (*Regardless of spoiling another's pleasure.*) Tink, the Wendy lives.

(TINK *gives expression to fury.*)

SECOND TWIN. (*Tell-tale.*) It was she who said that you wanted us to shoot the Wendy.

PETER. She said that? Then listen, Tink, I am your friend no more. (*There is a note of acerbity in* TINK'S *reply; it may mean "Who wants you?"*) Begone from me for ever. (*Now it is a very wet tinkle.*)

CURLY. She is crying.

TOOTLES. She says she is your fairy.

PETER. (*Who knows they are not worth worrying about.*) Oh well, not for ever, but for a whole week.

(TINK *goes off sulking, no doubt with the intention of giving all her friends an entirely false impression of* WENDY'S *appearance.*)

Now what shall we do with Wendy?

CURLY. Let us carry her down into the house.

SLIGHTLY. Ay, that is what one does with ladies.

PETER. No, you must not touch her; it wouldn't be sufficiently respectful.

SLIGHTLY. That is what I was thinking.

TOOTLES. But if she lies there she will die.

SLIGHTLY. Ay, she will die. It is a pity, but there is no way out.

PETER. Yes, there is. Let us build a house around her! (*Cheers again, meaning that no difficulty baffles* PETER.) Leave all to me. Bring the best of what we have. Gut our house. Be sharp. (*They race down their trees.*)

(*While* PETER *is engrossed in measuring* WENDY *so that the house may fit her,* JOHN *and* MICHAEL, *who have probably landed on the island with a bump, wander forward, so draggled and tired that if you were to ask* MICHAEL *whether he is awake or asleep he would probably answer: "I haven't tried yet."*)

MICHAEL. (*Bewildered.*) John, John, wake up. Where is Nana, John?

JOHN. (*With the help of one eye but not always the same eye.*) It is true, we did fly! (*Thankfully.*) And here is Peter. Peter, is this the place?

(PETER, *alas, has already forgotten them, as soon maybe he will forget* WENDY. *The first thing she should do now that she is here is to sew a handkerchief for him, and knot it as a jog to his memory.*)

PETER. (*Curtly.*) Yes.

MICHAEL. Where is Wendy? (PETER *points.*)

JOHN. (*Who still wears his hat.*) She is asleep.

MICHAEL. John, let us wake her and get her to make supper for us.

(*Some of the* BOYS *emerge, and he pinches one.*)

John, look at them!

PETER. (*Still house-building.*) Curly, see that these boys help in the building of the house.

JOHN. Build a house?

CURLY. For the Wendy.

JOHN. (*Feeling that there must be some mistake here.*)
For Wendy? Why, she is only a girl.

CURLY. That is why we are her servants.

JOHN. (*Dazed.*) Are you Wendy's servants?

PETER. Yes, and you also. Away with them. (*In another
moment they are woodsmen hacking at trees, with* CURLY
as overseer.) Slightly, fetch a doctor. (SLIGHTLY *reels
and goes. He returns professionally in* JOHN'S *hat.*) Please,
sir, are you a doctor?

SLIGHTLY. (*Trembling in his desire to give satisfaction.*)
Yes, my little man.

PETER. Please, sir, a lady lies very ill.

SLIGHTLY. (*Taking care not to fall over her.*) Tut, tut,
where does she lie?

PETER. In yonder glade. (*It is a variation of a game
they play.*)

SLIGHTLY. I will put a glass thing in her mouth. (*He
inserts an imaginary thermometer in* WENDY'S *mouth and
gives it a moment to record its verdict. He shakes it and
then consults it.*

PETER. (*Anxiously*). How is she?

SLIGHTLY. Tut, tut, this has cured her.

PETER. (*Leaping joyously.*) I am glad.

SLIGHTLY. I will call again in the evening. Give her
beef tea out of a cup with a spout to it, tut, tut.

(*The* BOYS *are running up with odd articles of furniture.*)

PETER. (*With an already fading recollection of the*
DARLING *nursery.*) These are not good enough for Wendy.
How I wish I knew the kind of house she would prefer!

FIRST TWIN. Peter, she is moving in her sleep.

TOOTLES. (*Opening* WENDY'S *mouth and gazing down
into the depths.*) Lovely!

PETER. Oh, Wendy, if you could sing the kind of house
you would like to have.

(*It is as if she had heard him.*)

WENDY. (*Without opening her eyes.*)
>I wish I had a woodland house,
>The littlest ever seen,
>With funny little red walls
>And roof of mossy green.

(*In the time she sings this and two other verses, such is the urgency of* PETER'S *silent orders that they have knocked down trees, laid a foundation and put up the walls and roof, so that she is now hidden from view.* "Windows," *cries* PETER, *and* CURLY *rushes them in,* "Roses," *and* TOOTLES *arrives breathless with a festoon for the door. Thus springs into existence the most delicious little house for beginners.*)

FIRST TWIN. I think it is finished.
PETER. There is no knocker on the door. (TOOTLES *hangs up the sole of his shoe.*) There is no chimney; we must have a chimney. (*They await his deliberations anxiously.*)
JOHN. (*Unwisely critical.*) It certainly does need a chimney.

(*He is again wearing his hat, which* PETER *seizes, knocks the top off it and places on the roof. In the friendliest way* SMOKE *begins to come out of the hat.*)

PETER. (*With his hand on the knocker.*) All look your best; the first impression is awfully important. (*He knocks, and after a dreadful moment of suspense, in which they cannot help wondering if anyone is inside, the door opens and who should come out but* WENDY! *She has evidently been tidying a little. She is quite surprised to find that she has nine children.*)
WENDY. (*Genteelly.*) Where am I?
SLIGHTLY. Wendy lady, for you we built this house.
NIBS AND TOOTLES. Oh, say you are pleased.
WENDY. (*Stroking the pretty thing.*) Lovely, darling house!

FIRST TWIN. And we are your children.

WENDY. (*Affecting surprise.*) Oh?

OMNES. (*Kneeling with outstretched arms.*) Wendy lady, be our mother! (*Now that they know it is pretend they acclaim her greedily.*)

WENDY. (*Not to make herself too cheap.*) Ought I? Of course it is frightfully fascinating; but you see I am only a little girl; I have no real experience.

OMNES. That doesn't matter. What we need is just a nice motherly person.

WENDY. Oh dear. I feel that is just exactly what I am.

OMNES. It is, it is, we saw it at once.

WENDY. Very well then, I will do my best. (*In their glee they go dancing obstreperously round the little house, and she sees that she must be firm with them as well as kind.*) Come inside at once, you naughty children, I am sure your feet are damp. And before I put you to bed I have just time to finish the story of Cinderella.

(*They all troop into the enchanting house, whose not least remarkable feature is that it holds them. A vision of* LIZA *passes, not perhaps because she has any right to be there; but she has so few pleasures and is so young that we just let her have a peep at the little house. By and by* PETER *comes out and marches up and down with drawn sword, for the* PIRATES *can be heard carousing far away on the lagoon, and the wolves are on the prowl. The little house, its walls so red and its roof so mossy, looks very cosy and safe, with a bright LIGHT showing through the blind, the chimney smoking beautifully, and* PETER *on guard. On our last sight of him it is so dark that we just guess he is the little figure who has fallen asleep by the door. DOTS OF LIGHT come and go. They are inquisitive fairies having a look at the house. Any other child in their way they would mischief, but they just tweak* PETER'S *nose and pass on. Fairies, you see, can touch him.*)

ACT III

THE MERMAIDS' LAGOON: *It is the end of a long playful day on the lagoon. The sun's rays have persuaded him to give them another five minutes, for one more race over the waters before he gathers them up and lets in the moon. There are many* MERMAIDS *here, going plop-plop, and one might attempt to count the tails did they not flash and disappear so quickly. At times a lovely* GIRL *leaps in the air seeking to get rid of her excess of scales, which fall in a silver shower as she shakes them off. From the coral grottoes beneath the lagoon, where are the* MERMAIDS'. *bed-chambers, comes fitful MUSIC.*

One of the most bewitching of these blue-eyed creatures is lying lazily on Marooner's Rock, combing her long tresses and noting effects in a transparent shell. PETER *and his* BAND *are in the water unseen behind the rock, whither they have tracked her as if she were a trout, and at a signal ten pairs of arms come whack upon the mermaid to enclose her. Alas, this is only what was meant to happen, for she hears the signal (which is the crow of a COCK) and slips through their arms into the water. It has been such a near thing that there are scales on some of their hands. They climb on to the rock crestfallen.*

WENDY. (*Preserving her scales as carefully as if they were rare postage stamps.*) I did so want to catch a mermaid.

PETER. (*Getting rid of his.*) It is awfully difficult to catch a mermaid.

(*The* MERMAIDS *at times find it just as difficult to catch him, though he sometimes joins them in their one game, which consists in lazily blowing their bubbles into the air and seeing who can catch them. The*

46

number of bubbles PETER *has flown away with!*
When the weather grows cold MERMAIDS *migrate to*
the other side of the world, and he once went with a
great shoal of them half the way.)

They are such cruel creatures, Wendy, that they try to
pull boys and girls like you into the water and drown
them.

WENDY. (*Too guarded by this time to ask what he*
means precisely by "like you," though she is very desirous
of knowing.) How hateful!

(*She is slightly different in appearance now, rather rounder,*
while JOHN *and* MICHAEL *are not quite so round.*
The reason is that when new lost children arrive
at his underground home PETER *finds new trees for*
them to go up and down by, and instead of fitting
the tree to them he makes them fit the tree. Some-
times it can be done by adding or removing garments,
but if you are bumpy, or the tree is an odd shape,
he has things done to you with a roller, and after
that you fit.
      The other BOYS *are now playing King of the*
Castle, throwing each other into the water, taking
headers and so on; but these two continue to talk.)

PETER. Wendy, this is a fearfully important rock. It is
called Marooner's Rock. Sailors are marooned, you know,
when their captain leaves them on a rock and sails away.
      WENDY. Leaves them on this little rock to drown?
      PETER. (*Lightly.*) Oh, they don't live long. Their hands
are tied, so that they can't swim. When the tide is full
this rock is covered with water, and then the sailor
drowns.

(WENDY *is uneasy as she surveys the rock, which is the*
only one in the lagoon and no larger than a table.
Since she last looked around a threatening change has
come over the scene. The sun has gone, but the moon

has not come. What has come is a cold shiver across the waters which has sent all the wiser MERMAIDS *to their coral recesses. They know that evil is creeping over the lagoon. Of the* BOYS PETER *is of course the first to scent it, and he has leapt to his feet before the words strike the rock—*

"And if we're parted by a shot
We're sure to meet below."

The games on the rock and around it end so abruptly that several DIVERS *are checked in the air. There they hang waiting for the word of command from* PETER. *When they get it they strike the water simultaneously, and the rock is at once as bare as if suddenly they had been blown off it. Thus the* PIRATES *find it deserted when their dinghy strikes the rock and is nearly stove in by the concussion.)*

SMEE. Luff, you spalpeen, luff! (*They are* SMEE *and* STARKEY, *with* TIGER LILY, *their captive, bound hand and foot.*) What we have got to do is to hoist the redskin on to the rock and leave her there to drown.

(*To one of her race this is an end darker than death by fire or torture, for it is written in the laws of the Piccaninnies that there is no path through water to the happy hunting ground. Yet her face is impassive; she is the daughter of a chief and must die as a chief's daughter; it is enough.*)

STARKEY. (*Chagrined because she does not mewl.*) No mewling. This is your reward for prowling round the ship with a knife in your mouth.

TIGER LILY. (*Stoically.*) Enough said.

SMEE. (*Who would have preferred a farewell palaver.*) So that's it! On to the rock with her, mate.

STARKEY. (*Experiencing for perhaps the last time the stirrings of a man.*) Not so rough, Smee; roughish, but not so rough.

SMEE. (*Dragging her on to the rock.*) It is the captain's orders.

(*A stave has in some past time been driven into the rock, probably to mark the burial place of hidden treasure, and to this they moor the dinghy.*)

WENDY. (*In the water.*) Poor Tiger Lily!

STARKEY. What was that? (*The* CHILDREN *bob.*)

PETER. (*Who can imitate the captain's voice so perfectly that even the author has a dizzy feeling that at times he was really* HOOK.) Ahoy there, you lubbers!

STARKEY. It is the captain; he must be swimming out to us.

SMEE. (*Calling.*) We have put the redskin on the rock, Captain.

PETER. Set her free.

SMEE. But Captain—

PETER. Cut her bonds, or I'll plunge my hook in you.

SMEE. This is queer!

STARKEY. (*Unmanned.*) Let us follow the captain's orders.

(*They undo the thongs and* TIGER LILY *slides between their legs into the lagoon, forgetting in her haste to utter her war-cry, but* PETER *utters it for her, so naturally that even the lost boys are deceived. It is at this moment that the voice of the true* HOOK *is heard.*)

HOOK. Boat ahoy!

SMEE. (*Relieved.*) It is the captain.

(HOOK *is swimming, and they help him to scale the rock. He is in gloomy mood.*)

STARKEY. Captain, is all well?

SMEE. He sighs.

STARKEY. He sighs again.

SMEE. (*Counting.*) And yet a third time he sighs. (*With foreboding.*) What's up, Captain?

HOOK. (*Who has perhaps found the large rich damp cake untouched.*) The game is up. Those boys have found a mother!

STARKEY. Oh evil day!

SMEE. What is a mother?

WENDY. (*Horrified.*) He doesn't know!

HOOK. (*Sharply.*) What was that?

(PETER *makes the splash of a mermaid's tail.*)

STARKEY. One of them mermaids.

HOOK. Dost not know, Smee? A mother is— (*He finds it more difficult to explain than he had expected, and looks about him for an illustration. He finds one in a great BIRD which drifts past in a nest as large as the roomiest basin.*) There is a lesson in mothers for you! The nest must have fallen into the water, but would the bird desert her eggs? (PETER, *who is now more or less off his head, makes the sound of a bird answering in the negative. The nest is borne out of sight.*)

STARKEY. Maybe she is hanging out here to protect Peter?

(HOOK'S *face clouds still further and* PETER *just manages not to call out that he needs no protection.*)

SMEE. (*Not usually a man of ideas.*) Captain, could we not kidnap these boys' mother and make her our mother?

HOOK. Obesity and bunions, 'tis a princely scheme. We will seize the children, make them walk the plank, and Wendy shall be our mother!

WENDY. Never! (*Another splash from* PETER.)

HOOK. What say you, bullies?

SMEE. There is my hand on 't.

STARKEY. And mine.

HOOK. And there is my hook. Swear. (*All swear.*) But I had forgot; where is the redskin?

SMEE. (*Shaken.*) That is all right, Captain; we let her go.

HOOK. (*Terrible.*) Let her go?

SMEE. 'Twas your own orders, Captain.

STARKEY. (*Whimpering.*) You called over the water to us to let her go.

HOOK. Brimstone and gall, what cozening is here? (*Disturbed by their faithful faces.*) Lads, I gave no such order.

SMEE. 'Tis passing queer.

HOOK. (*Addressing the immensities.*) Spirit that haunts this dark lagoon tonight, dost hear me?

PETER. (*In the same voice.*) Odds, bobs, hammer and tongs, I hear you.

HOOK. (*Gripping the stave for support.*) Who are you, stranger, speak.

PETER. (*Who is only too ready to speak.*) I am Jas Hook, Captain of the *Jolly Roger*.

HOOK. (*Now white to the gills.*) No, no, you are not.

PETER. Brimstone and gall, say that again and I'll cast anchor in you.

HOOK. If you are Hook, come tell me, who am I?

PETER. A codfish, only a codfish.

HOOK. (*Aghast.*) A codfish?

SMEE. (*Drawing back from him.*) Have we been captained all this time by a codfish?

STARKEY. It's lowering to our pride.

HOOK. (*Feeling that his ego is slipping from him.*) Don't desert me, bullies.

PETER. (*Top-heavy.*) Paw, fish, paw!

(*There is a touch of the feminine in* HOOK, *as in all the greatest pirates, and it prompts him to try the guessing game.*)

HOOK. Have you another name?

PETER. (*Falling to the lure.*) Ay, ay.

HOOK. (*Thirstily.*) Vegetable?

PETER. No.

HOOK. Mineral?

PETER. No.

HOOK. Animal?

PETER. (*After a hurried consultation with* TOOTLES.) Yes.

HOOK. Man?

PETER. (*With scorn.*) No.

HOOK. Boy?

PETER. Yes.

HOOK. Ordinary boy?

PETER. No!

HOOK. Wonderful boy?

PETER. (*To* WENDY'S *distress.*) Yes!

HOOK. Are you in England?

PETER. No.

HOOK. Are you here?

PETER. Yes.

HOOK. (*Beaten, though he feels he has very nearly got it.*) Smee, you ask him some questions.

SMEE. (*Rummaging his brains.*) I can't think of a thing.

PETER. Can't guess, can't guess! (*Foundering in his cockiness.*) Do you give it up?

HOOK. (*Eagerly.*) Yes.

PETER. All of you?

SMEE AND STARKEY. Yes.

PETER. (*Crowing.*) Well, then, I am Peter Pan!

(*Now they have him.*)

HOOK. Pan! Into the water, Smee. Starkey, mind the boat. Take him dead or alive!

PETER. (*Who still has all his baby teeth.*) Boys, lam into the pirates!

(*For a moment the only two we can see are in the dinghy, where* JOHN *throws himself on* STARKEY. STARKEY *wriggles into the lagoon and* JOHN *leaps so quickly after him that he reaches it first. The impression left on* STARKEY *is that he is being attacked by the* TWINS.

The water becomes stained. The dinghy drifts away. Here and there a head shows in the water, and once it is the head of the CROCODILE. *In the growing gloom some strike at their friends,* SLIGHTLY *getting* TOOTLES *in the fourth rib while he himself is pinked by* CURLY. *It looks as if the* BOYS *were getting the worse of it, which is perhaps just as well at this point, because* PETER, *who will be the determining factor in the end, has a perplexing way of changing sides if he is winning too easily.* HOOK'S *iron claw makes a circle of black water round him from which opponents flee like fishes. There is only one prepared to enter that dreadful circle. His name is* PAN. *Strangely, it is not in the water that they meet.* HOOK *has risen to the rock to breathe, and at the same moment* PETER *scales it on the opposite side. The rock is now wet and as slippery as a ball, and they have to crawl rather than climb. Suddenly they are face to face.* PETER *gnashes his pretty teeth with joy, and is gathering himself for the spring when he sees he is higher up the rock than his foe. Courteously he waits;* HOOK *sees his intention, and taking advantage of it claws twice.* PETER *is untouched, but unfairness is what he can never get used to, and in his bewilderment he rolls off the rock. The* CROCODILE, *whose tick has been drowned in the strife, rears its jaws, and* HOOK, *who has almost stepped into them, is pursued by it to land. All is quiet on the lagoon now, not a sound save little waves nibbling at the rock, which is smaller than when we last looked at it.* TWO BOYS *appear with the dinghy, and the* OTHERS *despite their wounds climb into it. They send the cry "Peter—Wendy" across the waters, but no answer comes.*)

NIBS. They must be swimming home.

JOHN. Or flying.

FIRST TWIN. Yes, that is it. Let us be off and call to them as we go.

(*The dinghy disappears with its load, whose hearts would sink it if they knew of the peril of* WENDY *and her captain. From near and far away come the cries "Peter—Wendy" till we no longer hear them.*

Two small figures are now on the rock. but they have fainted. A MERMAID *who has dared to come back in the stillness stretches up her arms and is slowly pulling* WENDY *into the water to drown her.* WENDY *starts up just in time.*)

WENDY. Peter!

(*He rouses himself and looks around him.*)

Where are we, Peter?

PETER. We are on the rock, but it is getting smaller. Soon the water will be over it. Listen!

(*They can hear the wash of the relentless little waves.*)

WENDY. We must go.

PETER. Yes.

WENDY. Shall we swim or fly?

PETER. Wendy, do you think you could swim or fly to the island without me?

WENDY. You know I couldn't, Peter; I am just a beginner.

PETER. Hook wounded me twice. (*He believes it; he is so good at pretend that he feels the pain, his arms hang limp.*) I can neither swim nor fly.

WENDY. Do you mean we shall both be drowned?

PETER. Look how the water is rising!

(*They cover their faces with their hands. Something touches* WENDY *as lightly as a kiss.*)

PETER. (*With little interest.*) It must be the tail of the kite we made for Michael; you remember it tore itself out of his hands and floated away. (*He looks up and sees the*

KITE sailing overhead.) The kite! Why shouldn't it carry you? (*He grips the tail and pulls, and the kite responds.*)
  WENDY. Both of us!
  PETER. It can't lift two. Michael and Curly tried.

(*She knows very well that if it can lift her it can lift him also, for she has been told by the boys as a deadly secret that one of the queer things about him is that he is no weight at all. But it is a forbidden subject.*)

  WENDY. I won't go without you. Let us draw lots which is to stay behind.
  PETER. And you a lady, never! (*The tail is in her hands, and the KITE is tugging hard. She holds out her mouth to PETER, but he knows they cannot do that.*) Ready, Wendy!

(*The KITE draws her out of sight across the lagoon.
    The WATERS are lapping over the rock now, and PETER knows that it will soon be submerged. Pale rays of LIGHT mingle with the moving clouds, and from the coral grottoes is to be heard a sound, at once the most musical and the most melancholy in the Never Land, the MERMAIDS calling to the moon to rise. PETER is afraid at last, and a tremor runs through him, like a shudder passing over the lagoon; but on the lagoon one shudder follows another till there are hundreds of them, and he feels just the one.*)

  PETER. (*With a drum beating in his breast as if he were a real boy at last.*) To die will be an awfully big adventure.

(*The BLIND rises again, and the lagoon is now suffused with MOONLIGHT. He is on the rock still, but the water is over his feet. The nest is borne nearer, and the BIRD, after cooing a message to him, leaves it and wings her way upwards. PETER, who knows the bird language, slips into the nest, first removing the two eggs and replacing them in* STARKEY'S *hat, which has been left on the stave. The HAT drifts away from the rock, but he uses the stave as a mast. The wind is driving him toward the open sea. He takes off his shirt, which he had forgotten to remove while bathing, and unfurls it as a sail. His vessel tacks, and he passes from sight, naked and victorious. The BIRD returns and sits on the hat.*)

ACT IV

THE HOME UNDER THE GROUND: *We see simultaneously the home under the ground with the* CHILDREN *in it and the wood above ground with the* REDSKINS *on it. Below, the* CHILDREN *are gobbling their evening meal; above, the* REDSKINS *are squatting in their blankets near the little house guarding the* CHILDREN *from the* PIRATES. *The only way of communicating between these two parties is by means of the hollow trees.*

The home has an earthen floor, which is handy for digging in if you want to go fishing; and owing to there being so many entrances there is not much wall space. The table at which the lost ones are sitting is a board on top of a live tree trunk, which has been cut flat but has such growing pains that the board rises as they eat, and they have sometimes to pause in their meals to cut a bit more off the trunk. Their seats are pumpkins or the large gay mushrooms of which we have seen an imitation one concealing the chimney. There is an enormous fireplace which is in almost any part of the room where you care to light it, and across this WENDY *has stretched strings, made of fibre, from which she hangs her washing. There are also various tom-fool things in the room of no use whatever.*

MICHAEL'S *basket bed is nailed high upon the wall as if to protect him from the cat, but there is no indication at present of where the others sleep. At the back between two of the tree trunks is a grindstone, and near it is a lovely hole, the size of a band-box, with a gay curtain drawn across so that you cannot see what is inside. This is* TINK'S *withdrawing-room and bed-chamber, and it is just as well that you cannot see inside, for it is so exquisite in its decoration and in the personal apparel spread out on the bed*

57

that you could scarcely resist making off with some-thing. TINK *is within at present, as one can guess from a GLOW showing through the chinks. It is her own glow, for though she has a chandelier for the look of the thing, of course she lights her residence herself. She is probably wasting valuable time just now wondering whether to put on the smoky blue or the apple-blossom.*

All the BOYS *except* PETER *are here, and* WENDY *has the head of the table, smiling complacently at their captivating ways, but doing her best at the same time to see that they keep the rules about hands-off-the-table, no-two-to-speak-at-once, and so on. She is wearing romantic woodland garments, sewn by her-self, with red berries in her hair which go charmingly with her complexion, as she knows; indeed she searched for red berries the morning after she reached the island. The* BOYS *are in picturesque attire of her contrivance, and if these don't always fit well the fault is not hers but the wearers', for they constantly put on each other's things when they put on any-thing at all.* MICHAEL *is in his cradle on the wall.* FIRST TWIN *is apart on a high stool and wears a dunce's cap, another invention of* WENDY'S, *but not wholly successful because everybody wants to be dunce.*

It is a pretend meal this evening, with nothing what-ever on the table, not a mug, nor a crust, nor a spoon. They often have these suppers and like them on occasions as well as the other kind, which consist chiefly of bread-fruit, tappa rolls, yams, mammee apples and banana splash, washed down with cala-bashes of poe-poe. The pretend meals are not WENDY'S *idea; indeed she was rather startled to find, on arriving, that* PETER *knew of no other kind, and she is not absolutely certain even now that he does eat the other kind, though no one appears to do it more heartily. He insists that the pretend meals*

*should be partaken of with gusto, and we see his
band doing their best to obey orders.*

WENDY. (*Her fingers to her ears, for their chatter and
clatter are deafening.*) Si-lence! Is your mug empty,
Slightly?

SLIGHTLY. (*Who would not say this if he had a mug.*)
Not quite empty, thank you.

NIBS. Mummy, he has not even begun to drink his poe-
poe.

SLIGHTLY. (*Seizing his chance, for this is tale-bearing.*)
I complain of Nibs!

(JOHN *holds up his hand.*)

WENDY. Well, John?

JOHN. May I sit in Peter's chair as he is not here?

WENDY. In your father's chair? Certainly not.

JOHN. He is not really our father. He did not even know
how to be a father till I showed him.

(*This is insubordination.*)

SECOND TWIN. I complain of John!

(*The gentle* TOOTLES *raises his hand.*)

TOOTLES. (*Who has the poorest opinion of himself.*) I
don't suppose Michael would let me be baby?

MICHAEL. No, I won't.

TOOTLES. May I be dunce?

FIRST TWIN. (*From his perch.*) No. It's awfully
difficult to be dunce.

TOOTLES. As I can't be anything important would any
of you like to see me do a trick?

OMNES. No.

TOOTLES. (*Subsiding.*) I hadn't really any hope.

(*The tale-telling breaks out again.*)

NIBS. Slightly is coughing on the table.

CURLY. The twins began with tappa rolls.

SLIGHTLY. I complain of Nibs!

NIBS. I complain of Slightly!

WENDY. Oh dear, I am sure I sometimes think that spinsters are to be envied.

MICHAEL. Wendy, I am too big for a cradle.

WENDY. You are the littlest, and a cradle is such a nice homely thing to have about a house. You others can clear away now. (*She sits down on a pumpkin near the fire to her usual evening occupation, darning.*) Every heel with a hole in it!

(*The* BOYS *clear away with dispatch, washing dishes they don't have in a non-existent sink and stowing them in a cupboard that isn't there. Instead of saving the table-leg tonight they crush it into the ground like a concertina, and are now ready for play, in which they indulge hilariously.*

A movement of the INDIANS *draws our attention to the scene above, Hitherto, with the exception of* PANTHER, *who sits on guard on top of the little house, they have been hunkering in their blankets, mute but picturesque; now all rise and prostrate themselves before the majestic figure of* PETER, *who approaches through the forest carrying a gun and game bag. It is not exactly a gun. He often wanders away alone with this weapon, and when he comes back you are never absolutely certain whether he has had an adventure or not. He may have forgotten it so completely that he says nothing about it; and then when you go out you find the body. On the other hand he may say a great deal about it, and yet you never find the body. Sometimes he comes home with his face scratched, and tells* WENDY, *as a thing of no importance, that he got these marks from the little people for cheeking them at a fairy wedding, and she listens politely, but she is never quite sure,*

*you know; indeed the only one who is sure about
anything on the island is* PETER.)

PETER. The Great White Father is glad to see the Piccaninny braves protecting his wigwam from the pirates.

TIGER LILY. The Great White Father save me from
pirates. Me his velly nice friend now; no let pirates hurt
him.

BRAVES. Ugh, ugh, wah!

TIGER LILY. Tiger Lily has spoken.

PANTHER. Loola, loola! Great Big Little Panther has
spoken.

PETER. It is well. The Great White Father has spoken.

(*This has a note of finality about it, with the implied
"And now shut up," which is never far from the
courteous receptions of well-meaning inferiors by
born leaders of men. He descends his tree, not un-
heard by* WENDY.)

start here

WENDY. Children, I hear your father's step. He likes
you to meet him at the door. (PETER *scatters pretend
nuts among them and watches sharply to see that they
crunch with relish.*) Peter, you just spoil them, you know!

JOHN. (*Who would be incredulous if he dare.*) Any
sport, Peter?

PETER. Two tigers and a pirate.

JOHN. (*Boldly.*) Where are their heads?

PETER. (*Contracting his little brows.*) In the bag.

JOHN. (*No, he doesn't say it. He backs away.*)

WENDY. (*Peeping into the bag.*) They are beauties!
(*She has learned her lesson.*)

FIRST TWIN. Mummy, we all want to dance.

WENDY. The mother of such an armful dance!

SLIGHTLY. As it is Saturday night?

(*They have long lost count of the days, but always if they
want to do anything special they say this is Saturday night, and then they do it.*)

WENDY. Of course it is Saturday night, Peter? (*He shrugs an indifferent assent.*) On with your nighties first.

(*They disappear into various recesses, and* PETER *and* WENDY *with her darning are left by the fire to dodder parentally. She emphasises it by humming a verse of "John Anderson my Jo," which has not the desired effect on* PETER. *She is too loving to be ignorant that he is not loving enough, and she hesitates like one who knows the answer to her question.*)

What is wrong, Peter?
    PETER. (*Scared.*) It is only pretend, isn't it, that I am their father?
    WENDY. (*Drooping.*) Oh yes.

(*His sigh of relief is without consideration for her feelings.*)

But they are ours, Peter, yours and mine.
    PETER. (*Determined to get at facts, the only things that puzzle him.*) But not really?
    WENDY. Not if you don't wish it.
    PETER. I don't.
    WENDY. (*Knowing she ought not to probe but driven to it by something within.*) What are your exact feelings for me, Peter?
    PETER. (*In the class-room.*) Those of a devoted son, Wendy.
    WENDY. (*Turning away.*) I thought so.
    PETER. You are so puzzling. Tiger Lily is just the same; there is something or other she wants to be to me, but she says it is not my mother.
    WENDY. (*With spirit.*) No, indeed it isn't.
    PETER. Then what is it?
    WENDY. It isn't for a lady to tell.

(*The curtain of the fairy chamber opens slightly, and* TINK, *who has doubtless been eavesdropping, tinkles a laugh of scorn.*)

PETER. (*Badgered.*) I suppose she means that she wants to be my mother.

(TINK'S *comment is "You silly ass."*)

WENDY. (*Who has picked up some of the fairy words.*) I almost agree with her!

START

(*The arrival of the* BOYS *in their nightgowns turns* WENDY'S *mind to practical matters, for the* CHILDREN *have to be arranged in line and passed or not passed for cleanliness.* SLIGHTLY *is the worst. At last we see how they sleep, for in a babel the great bed which stands on end by day against the wall is unloosed from custody and lowered to the floor. Though large, it is a tight fit for so many boys, and* WENDY *has made a rule that there is to be no turning round until one gives the signal, when all turn at once.*

FIRST TWIN *is the best dancer and performs mightily on the bed and in it and out of it and over it to an accompaniment of pillow fights by the less agile; and then there is a rush at* WENDY.)

NIBS. Now the story you promised to tell us as soon as we were in bed!

WENDY. (*Severely.*) As far as I can see you are not in bed yet.

(*They scramble into the bed, and the effect is as of a boxful of sardines.*)

WENDY. (*Drawing up her stool.*) Well, there was once a gentleman—

CURLY. I wish he had been a lady.

NIBS. I wish he had been a white rat.

WENDY. Quiet! There was a lady also. The gentleman's name was Mr. Darling and the lady's name was Mrs. Darling—

JOHN. I knew them!

MICHAEL. (*Who has been allowed to join the circle.*) I think I knew them.

WENDY. They were married, you know; and what do you think they had?

NIBS. White rats?

WENDY. No, they had three descendants. White rats are descendants also. Almost everything is a descendant. Now these three children had a faithful nurse called Nana.

MICHAEL. (*Alas.*) What a funny name!

WENDY. But Mr. Darling—(*Faltering.*) or was it Mrs. Darling?—was angry with her and chained her up in the yard; so all the children flew away. They flew away to the Never Land, where the lost boys are.

CURLY. I just thought they did; I don't know how it is, but I just thought they did.

TOOTLES. Oh, Wendy, was one of the lost boys called Tootles?

WENDY. Yes, he was.

TOOTLES. (*Dazzled.*) Am I in a story? Nibs, I am in a story!

PETER. (*Who is by the fire making Pan's pipes with his knife, and is determined that* WENDY *shall have fair play, however beastly a story he may think it.*) A little less noise there.

WENDY. (*Melting over the beauty of her present performance, but without any real qualms.*) Now I want you to consider the feelings of the unhappy parents with all their children flown away. Think, oh think, of the empty beds. (*The heartless ones think of them with glee.*)

FIRST TWIN. (*Cheerfully.*) It's awfully sad.

WENDY. But our heroine knew that her mother would always leave the window open for her progeny to fly back by; so they stayed away for years and had a lovely time.

(PETER *is interested at last.*)

FIRST TWIN. Did they ever go back?

WENDY. (*Comfortably.*) Let us now take a peep into the future. Years have rolled by, and who is this elegant lady of uncertain age alighting at London station?

(*The tension is unbearable.*)

NIBS. Oh, Wendy, who is she?

WENDY. (*Swelling.*) Can it be—yes—no—yes, it is the fair Wendy!

TOOTLES. I am glad.

WENDY. Who are the two noble portly figures accompanying her? Can they be John and Michael? They are. (*Pride of* MICHAEL.) "See, dear brothers," says Wendy, pointing upward, "there is the window standing open." So up they flew to their loving parents, and pen cannot inscribe the happy scene over which we draw a veil. (*Her triumph is spoilt by a groan from* PETER *and she hurries to him.*) Peter, what is it? (*Thinking he is ill, and looking lower than his chest.*) Where is it?

PETER. It isn't that kind of pain. Wendy, you are wrong about mothers. I thought like you about the window, so I stayed away for moons and moons, and then I flew back, but the window was barred, for my mother had forgotten all about me and there was another little boy sleeping in my bed.

(*This is a general damper.*)

JOHN. Wendy, let us go back!

WENDY. Are you sure mothers are like that?

PETER. Yes.

WENDY. John, Michael! (*She clasps them to her.*)

FIRST TWIN. (*Alarmed.*) You are not to leave us, Wendy?

WENDY. I must.

NIBS. Not tonight?

WENDY. At once. Perhaps mother is in half-mourning by this time! Peter, will you make the necessary arrangements?

(*She asks it in the steely tones women adopt when they are prepared secretly for opposition.*)

PETER. (*Coolly.*) If you wish it.

(*He ascends his tree to give the* REDSKINS *their instructions. The lost* BOYS *gather threateningly round* WENDY.)

CURLY. We won't let you go!
WENDY. (*With one of those inspirations women have, in an emergency, to make use of some male who need otherwise have no hope.*) Tootles, I appeal to you.
TOOTLES. (*Leaping to his death if necessary.*) I am just Tootles and nobody minds me, but the first who does not behave to Wendy I will blood him severely. (PETER *returns.*)
PETER. (*With awful serenity.*) Wendy, I told the braves to guide you through the wood as flying tires you so. Then Tinker Bell will take you across the sea. (*A shrill TINKLE from the boudoir probably means "and drop her into it".*)
NIBS. (*Fingering the curtain which he is not allowed to open.*) Tink, you are to get up and take Wendy on a journey. (*Star-eyed.*) She says she won't!
PETER. (*Taking a step toward that chamber.*) If you don't get up, Tink, and dress at once—She is getting up!
WENDY. (*Quivering now that the time to depart has come.*) Dear ones, if you will all come with me I feel almost sure I can get my father and mother to adopt you.

(*There is joy at this, not that they want parents, but novelty is their religion.*)

NIBS. But won't they think us rather a handful?
WENDY. (*A swift reckoner.*) Oh no, it will only mean having a few beds in the drawing-room; they can be hidden behind screens on first Thursdays.

(*Everything depends on* PETER.)

OMNES. Peter, may we go?
PETER. (*Carelessly through the pipes to which he is giving a finishing touch.*) All right.

(*They scurry off to dress for the adventure.*)

WENDY. (*Insinuatingly.*) Get your clothes, Peter.
PETER. (*Skipping about and playing fairy music on his pipes, the only music he knows.*) I am not going with you, Wendy.
WENDY. Yes, Peter!
PETER. No.

(*The* LOST ONES *run back gaily, each carrying a stick with a bundle on the end of it.*)

WENDY. Peter isn't coming!

(*All the faces go blank.*)

JOHN. (*Even* JOHN.) Peter not coming!
TOOTLES. (*Overthrown.*) Why, Peter?
PETER. (*His pipes more riotous than ever.*) I just want always to be a little boy and to have fun.

(*There is a general fear that they are perhaps making the mistake of their lives.*)

Now then, no fuss, no blubbering. (*With dreadful cynicism.*) I hope you will like your mothers! Are you ready, Tink? Then lead the way.

(TINK *darts up any tree, but she is the only one. The air above is suddenly rent with SHRIEKS and the clash of STEEL. Though they cannot see, the* BOYS *know that* HOOK *and his crew are upon the* INDIANS. *Mouths open and remain open, all in mute appeal to*

PETER. *He is the only boy on his feet now, a sword in his hand, the same he slew Barbicue with; and in his eye is the lust of battle.*

We can watch the carnage that is invisible to the CHILDREN. HOOK *has basely broken the two laws of Indian warfare, which are that the* REDSKINS *should attack first, and that it should be at dawn. They have known the* PIRATE *whereabouts since, early in the night, one of* SMEE'S *fingers crackled. The brushwood has closed behind their scouts as silently as the sand on the mole; for hours they have imitated the lonely call of the coyote; no stratagem has been overlooked, but, alas, they have trusted to the pale-faces' honour to await an attack at dawn, when his courage is known to be at the lowest ebb.* HOOK *falls upon them pell-mell, and one cannot withhold a reluctant admiration for the wit that conceived so subtle a scheme and the fell genius with which it is carried out. If the* BRAVES *would rise quickly they might still have time to scalp, but this they are forbidden to do by the traditions of their race, for it is written that they must never express surprise in the presence of the pale-face. For a brief space they remain recumbent, not a muscle moving, as if the foe were here by invitation. Thus perish the flower of the Piccannies, though not unavenged, for with* LEAN WOLF *fall* ALF MASON *and* CANARY ROBB, *while other pirates to bite dust are* BLACK GILMOUR *and* ALAN HERB, *that same* HERB *who is still remembered at Manaos for playing skittles with the mate of the* Switch *for each other's heads.* CHAY TURLEY, *who laughed with the wrong side of his mouth (having no other), is tomahawked by* PANTHER, *who eventually cuts a way through the shambles with* TIGER LILY *and a remnant of the tribe.*

→ TO P. 69

This onslaught passes and is gone like a fierce wind. The VICTOR'S *wipe their cutlasses, and squint, ferret-eyed, at their* LEADER. *He remains, as ever,*

Here

aloof in spirit and in substance. He signs to them to descend the trees, for he is convinced that PAN *is down there, and though he has smoked the bees it is the honey he wants. There is something in* PETER *that at all times goads this extraordinary man to frenzy; it is the boy's cockiness, which disturbs* HOOK *like an insect. If you have seen a lion in a cage futilely pursuing a sparrow you will know what is meant. The* PIRATES *try to do their captain's bidding, but the apertures prove to be not wide enough for them; he cannot even ram them down with a pole. He steals to the mouth of a tree and listens.*)

PETER. (*Prematurely.*) All is over! Here

WENDY. But who has won?

PETER. Hst! If the Indians have won they will beat the tom-tom; it is always their signal of victory.

(HOOK *licks his lips at this and signs to* SMEE, *who is sitting on it, to hold up the tom-tom. He beats upon it with his claws, and listens for results.*)

TOOTLES. The tom-tom!

PETER. (*Sheathing his sword.*) An Indian victory!

(*The CHEERS from below are music to the black hearts above.*)

You are quite safe now, Wendy. Boys, good-bye. (*He resumes his pipes.*)

WENDY. Peter, you will remember about changing your flannels, won't you?

PETER. Oh, all right!

WENDY. And this is your medicine.

(*She puts something into a shell and leaves it on a ledge between two of the trees. It is only water, but she measures it out in drops.*)

PETER. I won't forget.
WENDY. Peter, what are you to me?
PETER. (*Through the pipes.*) Your son, Wendy.
WENDY. Oh, good-bye!

(*The* TRAVELLERS *start upon their journey, little witting that* HOOK *has issued his silent orders: a* MAN *to the mouth of each tree, and a row of* MEN *between the trees and the little house. As the* CHILDREN *squeeze up they are plucked from their trees, trussed, thrown like bales of cotton from one* PIRATE *to another, and so piled up in the little house. The only one treated differently is* WENDY, *whom* HOOK *escorts to the house on his arm with hateful politeness. He signs to his* DOGS *to be gone, and they depart through the wood, carrying the little house with its strange merchandise and singing their ribald song. The chimney of the little house emits a jet of* SMOKE *fitfully, as if not sure what it ought to do just now.*

HOOK *and* PETER *are now, as it were, alone on the island. Below,* PETER *is on the bed, asleep, no weapon near him; above,* HOOK, *armed to the teeth, is searching noiselessly for some tree down which the nastiness of him can descend. Don't be too much alarmed by this; it is precisely the situation* PETER *would have chosen; indeed if the whole thing were pretend—. One of his arms droops over the edge of the bed, a leg is arched, and the mouth is not so tightly closed that we cannot see the little pearls. He is dreaming, and in his dreams he is always in pursuit of a boy who was never here, nor anywhere: the only boy who could beat him.*

HOOK *finds the tree. It is the one set apart for* SLIGHTLY, *who being addicted when hot to the drinking of water has swelled in consequence and surreptitiously scooped his tree for easier descent and egress. Down this the* PIRATE *wriggles a passage. In the aperture below his face emerges and goes green as he glares at the sleeping* CHILD. *Does no feeling*

*of compassion disturb his sombre breast? The man is
not wholly evil: he has a* Thesaurus *in his cabin,
and is no mean performer on the flute. What really
warps him is a presentiment that he is about to fail.
This is not unconnected with a beatific smile on the
face of the sleeper, whom he cannot reach owing to
being stuck at the foot of the tree. He, however, sees
the medicine shell within easy reach, and to* WENDY'S
*draught he adds from a bottle five drops of poison
distilled when he was weeping from the red in his
eye. The expression on* PETER'S *face merely implies
that something heavenly is going on.* HOOK *worms
his way upwards, and winding his cloak around him,
as if to conceal his person from the night of which he
is the blackest part, he stalks moodily towards the
lagoon.*

*A dot of LIGHT flashes past him and darts down
the nearest tree, looking for* PETER, *only for* PETER,
*quite indifferent about the others when she finds him
safe.*)

PETER. (*Stirring.*) Who is that? (TINK *has to tell her
tale, in one long ungrammatical sentence.*) The redskins
were defeated? Wendy and the boys captured by the
pirates! I'll rescue her, I'll rescue her! (*He leaps first at
his dagger, and then at his grindstone, to sharpen it.* TINK
alights near the shell, and rings out a warning cry.) Oh,
that is just my medicine. Poisoned? Who could have
poisoned it? I promised Wendy to take it, and I will as
soon as I have sharpened my dagger. (TINK, *who sees its
red colour and remembers the red in the* PIRATE'S *eye,
nobly swallows the draught as* PETER'S *hand is reaching
for it.*) Why, Tink, you have drunk my medicine! (*She
flutters strangely about the room, answering him now in a
very thin tinkle.*) It was poisoned and you drank it to
save my life! Tink, dear Tink, are you dying? (*He has
never called her dear Tink before, and for a moment she
is gay; she alights on his shoulder, gives his chin a loving
bite, whispers "You silly ass," and falls on her tiny bed.*

The boudoir, which is lit by her, flickers ominously. He is on his knees by the opening.)

Her light is growing faint, and if it goes out, that means she is dead! Her voice is so low I can scarcely tell what she is saying. She says—she says she thinks she could get well again if children believed in fairies! (*He rises and throws out his arms he knows not to whom, perhaps to the boys and girls of whom he is not one.*) Do you believe in fairies? Say quick that you believe! If you believe, clap your hands! (*Many clap, some don't, a few hiss. Then perhaps there is a rush of* NANAS *to the nurseries to see what on earth is happening. But* TINK *is saved.*) Oh, thank you, thank you, thank you! And now to rescue Wendy!

(TINK *is already as merry and impudent as a grig, with not a thought for those who have saved her.* PETER *ascends his tree as if he were shot up it. What he is feeling is "Hook or me this time!" He is frightfully happy. He soon hits the trail, for the smoke from the little house has lingered here and there to guide him. He takes wing.*)

ACT V

Scene I

The Pirate Ship: *The stage directions for the opening of this scene are as follows:—1 Circuit Amber checked to 80. Battens, all Amber checked, 3 ship's lanterns alight, Arcs: prompt perch 1. Open dark amber flooding back, O.P. perch open dark amber flooding upper deck. Arc on tall steps at back of cabin to flood back cloth. Open dark Amber. Warning for slide. Plank ready. Call* Hook.

In the strange light thus described we see what is happening on the deck of the Jolly Roger, *which is flying the skull and crossbones and lies low in the water. There is no need to call* Hook, *for he is here already, and indeed there is not a pirate aboard who would dare to call him. Most of them are at present carousing in the bowels of the vessel, but on the poop* Mullins *is visible, in the only great-coat on the ship, raking with his glass the monstrous rocks within which the lagoon is cooped. Such a look-out is supererogatory, for the pirate craft floats immune in the horror of her name.*

From Hook's *cabin at the back* Starkey *appears and leans over the bulwark, silently surveying the sullen waters. He is bare-headed and is perhaps thinking with bitterness of his hat, which he sometimes sees still drifting past him with the Never bird sitting on it. The* Black Pirate *is asleep on deck, yet even in his dreams rolling mechanically out of the way when* Hook *draws near. The only sound to be heard is made by* Smee *at his sewing-machine, which lends a touch of domesticity to the night.*

Hook *is now leaning against the mast, now prowling the deck, the double cigar in his mouth. With* Peter *surely at last removed from his path we,*

73

who know how vain a tabernacle is man, would not
be surprised to find him bellied out by the winds of
his success, but it is not so; he is still uneasy, look-
ing long and meaninglessly at familiar objects, such
as the ship's bell or the Long Tom, like one who
may shortly be a stranger to them. It is as if Pan's
terrible oath "Hook or me this time!" had already
boarded the ship.

HOOK. (*Communing with his ego.*) How still the night
is; nothing sounds alive. Now is the hour when children
in their homes are a-bed; their lips bright-browned with
the good-night chocolate, and their tongues drowsily
searching for belated crumbs housed insecurely on their
shining cheeks. Compare with them the children on this
boat about to walk the plank. Split my infinitives, but 'tis
my hour of triumph! (*Clinging to this fair prospect he
dances a few jubilant steps, but they fall below his usual
form.*) And yet some disky spirit compels me now to
make my dying speech, lest when dying there may be no
time for it. All mortals envy me, yet better perhaps for
Hook to have had less ambition! O fame, fame, thou
glittering bauble, what if the very—(SMEE, *engrossed in
his labours at the sewing-machine, tears a piece of calico
with a rending sound which makes the Solitary think for
a moment that the untoward has happened to his garments.*) No little children love me. I am told they play at
Peter Pan, and that the strongest always chooses to be
Peter. They would rather be a Twin than Hook; they
force the baby to be Hook. The baby! that is where the
canker gnaws. (*He contemplates his industrious* BOAT-
SWAIN.) 'Tis said they find Smee lovable. But an hour
agone I found him letting the youngest of them try on his
spectacles. Pathetic Smee, the Nonconformist pirate, a
happy smile upon his face because he thinks they fear
him! How can I break it to him that they think him
lovable? No, bi-carbonate of Soda, no, not even—
(*Another rending of the calico disturbs him, and he has
a private consultation with* STARKEY, *who turns him round*

and evidently assures him that all is well. The peroration of his speech is nevertheless for ever lost, as EIGHT BELLS strikes and his CREW *pour forth in bacchanalian orgy. From the poop he watches their dance till it frets him beyond bearing.*) Quiet, you dogs, or I'll cast anchor in you! (*He descends to a barrel on which there are playing-cards, and his* CREW *stand waiting, as ever, like whipped curs.*) Are all the prisoners chained, so that they can't fly away?

JUKES. Ay, ay, Captain.

HOOK. Then hoist them up.

STARKEY. (*Raising the door of the hold.*) Tumble up, you ungentlemanly lubbers.

(*The terrified* BOYS *are prodded up and tossed about the deck.* HOOK *seems to have forgotten them; he is sitting by the barrel with his cards.*)

HOOK. (*Suddenly.*) So! Now then, you bullies, six of you walk the plank tonight, but I have room for two cabin-boys. Which of you is it to be? (*He returns to his cards.*)

TOOTLES. (*Hoping to soothe him by putting the blame on the only person vaguely remembered, who is always willing to act as a buffer.*) You see, sir, I don't think my mother would like me to be a pirate. Would your mother like you to be a pirate, Slightly?

SLIGHTLY. (*Implying that otherwise it would be a pleasure to him to oblige.*) I don't think so. Twin, would your mother like—

HOOK. Stow this gab. (*To* JOHN.) You boy, you look as if you had a little pluck in you. Didst never want to be a pirate, my hearty?

JOHN. (*Dazzled by being singled out.*) When I was at school—what do you think, Michael?

MICHAEL. (*Stepping into prominence.*) What would you call me if I joined?

HOOK. Blackbeard Joe.

MICHAEL. John, what do you think?

JOHN. Stop, should we still be respectful subjects of King George?

HOOK. You would have to swear "Down with King George."

JOHN. (*Grandly.*) Then I refuse!

MICHAEL. And I refuse.

HOOK. That seals your doom. Bring up their mother.

(WENDY *is driven up from the hold and thrown to him. She sees at the first glance that the deck has not been scrubbed for years.*)

So, my beauty, you are to see your children walk the plank.

WENDY. (*With noble calmness.*) Are they to die?

HOOK. They are. Silence all, for a mother's last words to her children.

WENDY. These are my last words. Dear boys, I feel that I have a message to you from your real mothers, and it is this, "We hope our sons will die like English gentlemen."

(*The* BOYS *go on fire.*)

TOOTLES. I am going to do what my mother hopes. What are you to do, Twin?

FIRST TWIN. What my mother hopes. John, what are—

HOOK. Tie her up! Get the plank ready.

(WENDY *is roped to the mast; but no one regards her, for all eyes are fixed upon the plank now protruding from the poop over the ship's side. A great change, however, occurs in the time* HOOK *takes to raise his claw and point to this deadly engine. No one is now looking at the plank: for the tick, tick of the* CROC-ODILE *is heard. Yet it is not to bear on the* CROCODILE *that all eyes slew round, it is that they may bear on* HOOK. *Otherwise prisoners and captors are equally inert, like actors in some play who have found themselves "on" in a scene in which they are not per-*)

*sonally concerned. Even the iron claw hangs inactive,
as if aware that the* CROCODILE *is not coming for it.
Affection for their captain, now cowering from view,
is not what has given* HOOK *his dominance over the
crew, but as the menacing sound draws nearer they
close their eyes respectfully.*

There is no crocodile. It is PETER, *who has been
circling the pirate ship, ticking as he flies far more
superbly than any clock. He drops into the water and
climbs aboard, warning the captives with upraised
finger [but still ticking] not for the moment to give
audible expression to their natural admiration. Only
one* PIRATE *sees him,* WHIBBLES *of the eye patch,
who comes up from below.* JOHN *claps a hand on*
WHIBBLES' *mouth to stifle the groan;* FOUR BOYS
hold him to prevent the thud; PETER *delivers the
blow, and the carrion is thrown overboard. "One!"
says* SLIGHTLY, *beginning to count.*

STARKEY is the first PIRATE *to open his eyes. The
ship seems to him to be precisely as when he closed
them. He cannot interpret the sparkle that has come
into the faces of the captives, who are cleverly pre-
tending to be as afraid as ever. He little knows that
the door of the dark cabin has just closed on one
more* BOY. *Indeed it is for* HOOK *alone he looks, and
he is a little surprised to see him.*)

STARKEY. (*Hoarsely.*) It is gone, Captain! There is not
a sound.

(*The tenement that is* HOOK *heaves tumultuously and he
is himself again.*)

HOOK. (*Now convinced that some fair spirit watches
over him.*) Then here is to Johnny Plank—
                Avast, belay, the English brig
                We took and quickly sank,
                And for a warning to the crew
                We made them walk the plank!

(*As he sings he capers detestably along an imaginary plank and his copy-cats do likewise, joining in the chorus.*)

> Yo ho, yo ho, the frisky cat,
> You walks along it so.
> Till it goes down and you goes down
> To tooral looral lo!

(*The brave* CHILDREN *try to stem this monstrous torrent by breaking into the National Anthem.*)

STARKEY. (*Paling.*) I don't like it, messmates!

HOOK. Stow that, Starkey. Do you boys want a touch of the cat before you walk the plank? (*He is more pitiless than ever now that he believes he has a charmed life.*) Fetch the cat, Jukes; it is in the cabin.

JUKES. Ay, ay, sir. (*It is one of his commonest remarks, and is only recorded now because he never makes another. The stage direction "Exit* JUKES" *has in this case a special significance. But only the* CHILDREN *know that someone is awaiting this unfortunate in the cabin, and* HOOK *tramples them down as he resumes his ditty*:)

HOOK. Yo ho, yo ho, the scratching cat
> Its tails are nine you know,
> And when they're writ upon your back,
> You're fit to—

(*The last words will ever remain a matter of conjecture, for from the dark cabin comes a curdling SCREECH which wails through the ship and dies away. It is followed by a SOUND, almost more eerie in the circumstances, that can only be likened to the crowing of a cock.*)

HOOK. What was that?

SLIGHTLY. (*Solemnly.*) Two!

(CECCO *swings into the cabin, and in a moment returns, livid.*)

HOOK. (*With an effort.*) What is the matter with Bill Jukes, you dog?

CECCO. The matter with him is he is dead—stabbed.

PIRATES. Bill Jukes dead!

CECCO. The cabin is as black as a pit, but there is something terrible in there: the thing you heard a-crowing.

HOOK. (*Slowly.*) Cecco, go back and fetch me out that doodle-doo.

CECCO. (*Unstrung.*) No, Captain, no. (*He supplicates on his knees, but his* MASTER *advances on him implacably.*)

HOOK. (*In his most syrupy voice.*) Did you say you would go, Cecco?

(CECCO *goes.* ALL *listen. There is one SCREECH, one CROW.*)

SLIGHTLY. (*As if he were a bell tolling.*) Three!

HOOK. 'Sdeath and oddfish, who is to bring me out that doodle-doo?

(*No one steps forward.*)

STARKEY. (*Injudiciously.*) Wait till Cecco comes out.

(*The black looks of some others encourage him.*)

HOOK. I think I heard you volunteer, Starkey.

STARKEY. (*Emphatically.*) No, by thunder!

HOOK. (*In that syrupy voice which might be more engaging when accompanied by his flute.*) My hook thinks you did. I wonder if it would not be advisable, Starkey, to humour the hook?

STARKEY. I'll swing before I go in there.

HOOK. (*Gleaming.*) Is it mutiny? Starkey is ringleader. Shake hands, Starkey.

STARKEY *recoils from the claw. It follows him till he leaps overboard.*)

Did any other gentleman say mutiny?

(*They indicate that they did not even know the late* STAR-
      KEY.)

SLIGHTLY. Four!
HOOK. I will bring out that doodle-doo myself.

(*He raises a blunderbuss but casts it from him with a
      menacing gesture which means that he has more faith
      in the claw. With a lighted lantern in his hand he
      enters the cabin. Not a sound is to be heard now on
      the ship, unless it be* SLIGHTLY *wetting his lips to
      say* "*Five.*" HOOK *staggers out.*)

HOOK. (*Unsteadily.*) Something blew out the light.
MULLINS. (*With dark meaning.*) Some—thing?
NOODLER. What of Cecco?
HOOK. He is as dead as Jukes.

(*They are superstitious like all sailors, and* MULLINS *has
      planted a dire conception in their minds.*)

COOKSON. They do say as the surest sign a ship's
accurst is when there is one aboard more than can be
accounted for.
NOODLER. I've heard he allus boards the pirate craft
at last. (*With dreadful significance.*) Has he a tail,
Captain?
MULLINS. They say that when he comes it is in the like-
ness of the wickedest man aboard.
COOKSON. (*Clinching it.*) Has he a hook, Captain?

(*Knives and pistols come to hand, and there is a general
      cry* "*The ship is doomed!*" *But it is not his dogs that
      can frighten* JAS HOOK. *Hearing something like a
      cheer from the* BOYS *he wheels round, and his face
      brings them to their knees.*)

HOOK. So you like it, do you! By Caius and Balbus,

bullies, here is a notion: open the cabin door and drive
them in. Let them fight the doodle-doo for their lives. If
they kill him we are so much the better; if he kills them
we are none the worse.

(*This masterly stroke restores their confidence; and the*
BOYS, *affecting fear, are driven into the cabin.
Desperadoes though the* PIRATES *are, some of them
have been boys themselves, and all turn their backs
to the cabin and listen, with arms outstretched to it
as if to ward off the horrors that are being enacted
there.*

Relieved by PETER *of their manacles, and armed
with such weapons as they can lay their hands on, the*
BOYS *steal out softly as snowflakes, and under their*
CAPTAIN'S *hushed order find hiding-places on the
poop. He releases* WENDY; *and now it would be easy
for them all to fly away, but it is to be* HOOK *or him
this time. He signs to her to join the others, and
with awful grimness folding her cloak around him,
the hood over his head, he takes her place by the
mast, and crows.*)

MULLINS. The doodle-doo has killed them all!
SEVERAL. The ship's bewitched.

(*They are snapping at* HOOK *again.*)

HOOK. I've thought it out, lads; there is a Jonah
aboard.
SEVERAL. (*Advancing upon him.*) Ay, a man with a
hook.

(*If he were to withdraw one step their knives would be in
him, but he does not flinch.*)

HOOK. (*Temporising.*) No, lads, no, it is the girl. Never
was luck on a pirate ship wi' a woman aboard. We'll
right the ship when she has gone.

MULLINS. (*Lowering his cutlass.*) It's worth trying.

HOOK. Throw the girl overboard.

MULLINS. (*Jeering.*) There is none can save you now, missy.

PETER. There is one.

MULLINS. Who is that?

PETER. (*Casting off the cloak.*) Peter Pan, the avenger!

(*He continues standing there to let the effect sink in.*)

HOOK. (*Throwing out a suggestion.*) Cleave him to the brisket.

(*But he has a sinking that this boy has no brisket.*)

NOODLER. The ship's accurst!

PETER. Down, boys, and at them!

(*The* BOYS *leap from their concealment and the clash of arms resound through the vessel. Man to man the* PIRATES *are the stronger, but they are unnerved by the suddenness of the onslaught and they scatter, thus enabling their opponents to hunt in couples and choose their quarry. Some are hurled into the lagoon; others are dragged from dark recesses. There is no* BOY *whose weapon is not reeking save* SLIGHTLY, *who runs about with a lantern, counting, ever counting.*) To P. 84

WENDY. (*Meeting* MICHAEL *in a moment's lull.*) Oh, Michael, stay with me, protect me!

MICHAEL. (*Reeling.*) Wendy, I've killed a pirate!

WENDY. It's awful, awful.

MICHAEL. No, it isn't, I like it, I like it.

(*He casts himself into the group of* BOYS *who are encircling* HOOK. *Again and again they close upon him and again and again he hews a clear space.*)

HOOK. Back, back, you mice. It's Hook; do you like

him? (*He lifts up* MICHAEL *with his claw and uses him as a buckler. A terrible voice breaks in.*)

PETER. Put up your swords, boys. This man is mine.

HOOK *shakes* MICHAEL *off his claw as if he were a drop of water, and these two antagonists face each other for their final bout. They measure swords at arms' length, make a sweeping motion with them, and bringing the points to the deck rest their hands upon the hilts.*)

HOOK. (*With curling lip.*) So, Pan, this is all your doing!

PETER. Ay, Jas Hook, it is all my doing.

HOOK. Proud and insolent youth, prepare to meet thy doom.

PETER. Dark and sinister man, have at thee.

(*Some say that he had to ask* TOOTLES *whether the word was sinister or canister.*)

HOOK *or* PETER *this time! They fall to without another word.* PETER *is a rare swordsman, and parries with dazzling rapidity, sometimes before the other can make his stroke.* HOOK, *if not quite so nimble in wrist play, has the advantage of a yard or two in reach, but though they close he cannot give the quietus with his claw, which seems to find nothing to tear at. He does not, especially in the most heated moments, quite see* PETER, *who to his eyes, now blurred or opened clearly for the first time, is less like a boy than a mote of dust dancing in the sun. By some impalpable stroke* HOOK'S *sword is whipped from his grasp, and when he stoops to raise it a little foot is on its blade. There is no deep gash on* HOOK, *but he is suffering torment as from innumerable jags.*)

BOYS. (*Exulting.*) Now, Peter, now!

(PETER *raises the sword by its blade, and with an inclina-*

tion of the head that is perhaps slightly overdone, presents the hilt to his enemy.)

HOOK. 'Tis some fiend fighting me! Pan, who and what art thou?

(The CHILDREN *listen eagerly for the answer, none quite so eagerly as* WENDY.)

PETER. (*At a venture.*) I'm youth, I'm joy, I'm a little bird that has broken out of the egg.
HOOK. To 't again!

(He has now a damp feeling that this boy is the weapon which is to strike him from the lists of man; but the grandeur of his mind still holds and, true to the traditions of his flag, he fights on like a human flail. PETER *flutters round and through and over these gyrations as if the wind of them blew him out of the danger zone, and again and again he darts in and jags.)*

Here HOOK. (*Stung to madness.*) I'll fire the powder magazine. (*He disappears they know not where.*)
CHILDREN. Peter, save us!

*(*PETER, *alas, goes the wrong way and* HOOK *returns.)*

HOOK. (*Sitting on the hold with gloomy satisfaction.*) In two minutes the ship will be blown to pieces.

(They cast themselves before him in entreaty.)

CHILDREN. Mercy, mercy!
HOOK. Back, you pewling spawn. I'll show you now the road to dusty death. A holocaust of children, there is something grand in the idea!

*(*PETER *appears with the smoking bomb in his hand and*

Finish

tosses it overboard. HOOK *has not really had much hope, and he rushes at his other persecutors with his head down like some exasperated bull in the ring; but with bantering cries they easily elude him by flying among the rigging.*

Where is PETER? *The incredible boy has apparently forgotten the recent doings, and is sitting on a barrel playing upon his pipes. This may surprise others but does not surprise* HOOK. *Lifting a blunderbuss he strikes forlornly not at the* BOY *but at the barrel, which is hurled across the deck.* PETER *remains sitting in the air still playing upon his pipes. At this sight the great heart of* HOOK *breaks. That not wholly unheroic figure climbs the bulwarks murmuring* "Floreat Etona," *and prostrates himself into the water, where the* CROCODILE *is waiting for him open-mouthed.* HOOK *knows the purpose of this yawning cavity, but after what he has gone through he enters it like one greeting a friend.*

The CURTAIN *rises to show* PETER *a very Napoleon on his ship. It must not rise again lest we see him on the poop in* HOOK'S *hat and cigars, and with a small iron claw.*)

ACT FIVE

SCENE 2

THE NURSERY AND THE TREE-TOPS: *The old nursery appears again with everything just as it was at the beginning of the play, except that the kennel has gone and that the window is standing open. So* PETER *was wrong about mothers; indeed there is no subject on which he is so likely to be wrong.*

MRS. DARLING *is asleep on a chair near the window her eyes tired with searching the heavens.* NANA *is stretched out listless on the floor. She is the cynical one, and though custom has made her hang the* CHILD-

REN'S *night things on the fire-guard for an airing,
she surveys them not hopefully but with some self-
contempt.*

MRS. DARLING. (*Starting up as if we had whispered to
her that her brats are coming back.*) Wendy, John, Michael!
(NANA *lifts a sympathetic paw to the poor soul's lap.*)
I see you have put their night things out again, Nana!
It touches my heart to watch you do that night after
night. But they will never come back.

(*In trouble the difference of station can be completely
ignored, and it is not strange to see these two using
the same handkerchief. Enter LIZA, who in the gentle-
ness with which the house has been run of late is perhaps a little more masterful than of yore.*)

LIZA. (*Feeling herself degraded by the announcement.*)
Nana's dinner is served.

(NANA, *who quite understands what are LIZA's feelings,
departs for the dining-room with our exasperating
leisureliness, instead of running, as we would all do if
we followed our instincts.*)

LIZA. To think I have a master as have changed places
with his dog!
MRS. DARLING. (*Gently.*) Out of remorse, Liza.
LIZA. (*Surely exaggerating.*) I am a married woman
myself. I don't think it's respectable to go to his office in
a kennel, with the street boys running alongside cheering.
(*Even this does not rouse her mistress, which may have
been the honourable intention.*) There, that is the cab
fetching him back! (*Amid interested CHEERS from the
street the kennel is conveyed to its old place by a CABBY
and FRIEND, and MR. DARLING scrambles out of it in his
office clothes.*)
MR. DARLING. (*Giving her his hat loftily.*) If you will
be so good, Liza. (*The cheering is resumed.*) It is very
gratifying!

LIZA. (*Contemptuous.*) Lot of little boys.

MR. DARLING. (*With the new sweetness of one who has sworn never to lose his temper again.*) There were several adults today.

(*She goes off scornfully with the hat and the* TWO MEN, *but he has not a word of reproach for her. It ought to melt us when we see how humbly grateful he is for a kiss from his* WIFE, *so much more than he feels he deserves. One may think he is wrong to exchange into the kennel, but sorrow has taught him that he is the kind of man who whatever he does contritely he must do to excess; otherwise he soon abandons doing it.*)

MRS. DARLING. (*Who has known this for quite a long time.*) What sort of a day have you had, George?

(*He is sitting on the floor by the kennel.*)

MR. DARLING. There were never less than a hundred running round the cab cheering, and when we passed the Stock Exchange the members came out and waved.

(*He is exultant but uncertain of himself, and with a word she could dispirit him utterly.*)

MRS. DARLING. (*Bravely.*) I am so proud, George.

MR. DARLING. (*Commendation from the nearest quarter ever going to his head.*) I have been put on a picture postcard, dear.

MRS. DARLING. (*Nobly.*) Never!

MR. DARLING. (*Thoughtlessly.*) Ah, Mary, we should not be such celebrities if the children hadn't flown away.

MRS. DARLING. (*Startled.*) George, you are sure you are not enjoying it?

MR. DARLING. (*Anxiously.*) Enjoying it! See my punishment: living in a kennel.

MRS. DARLING. Forgive me, dear one.

MR. DARLING. It is I who need forgiveness, always I, never you. And now I feel drowsy. (*He retires into the kennel.*) Won't you play me to sleep on the nursery piano? And shut that window, Mary dearest; I feel a draught.

MRS. DARLING. Oh, George, never ask me to do that. The window must always be left open for them, always, always.

(*She goes into the day nursery, from which we presently hear her playing the sad song of Margaret. She little knows that her last remark has been overheard by a* BOY *crouching at the window. He steals into the room accompanied by a ball of LIGHT.*)

PETER. Tink, where are you? Quick, close the window. (*It closes.*) Bar it. (*The bar slams down.*) Now when Wendy comes she will think her mother has barred her out, and she will have to come back to me! (TINKER BELL *sulks.*) Now, Tink, you and I must go out by the door. (*Doors, however, are confusing things to those who are used to windows, and he is puzzled when he finds that this one does not open on to the firmament. He tries the other, and sees the piano player.*) It is Wendy's mother! (TINK *pops on to his shoulder and they keep together.*) She is a pretty lady, but not so pretty as my mother. (*This is a pure guess.*) She is making the box say "Come home, Wendy." You will never see Wendy again, lady, for the window is barred! (*He flutters about the room joyously like a bird, but has to return to that door.*) She has laid her head down on the box. There are two wet things sitting on her eyes. As soon as they go away another two come and sit on her eyes. (*She is heard moaning, "Wendy, Wendy, Wendy."*) She wants me to unbar the window. I won't! She is awfully fond of Wendy. I am fond of her too. We can't both have her, lady! (*A funny feeling comes over him.*) Come on, Tink; we don't want any silly mothers.

(*He opens the window and they fly out.*)

*It is thus that the truants find entrance easy when
they alight on the sill,* JOHN *to his credit having the
tired* MICHAEL *on his shoulders. They have nothing
else to their credit; no compunction for what they
have done, not the tiniest bit of fear that any just person
may be awaiting them with a stick. The* YOUNGEST
is in a daze, but the TWO OTHERS *are shining vir-
tuously like holy people who are about to give two
other people a treat.*)

MICHAEL. (*Looking about him.*) I think I have been
here before.

JOHN. It's your home, you stupid.

WENDY. There is your old bed, Michael.

MICHAEL. I had nearly forgotten.

JOHN. I say, the kennel!

WENDY. Perhaps Nana is in it.

JOHN. (*Peering.*) There is a man asleep in it.

WENDY. (*Remembering him by the bald patch.*) It's
father!

JOHN. So it is!

MICHAEL. Let me see father. (*Disappointed.*) He is not
as big as the pirate I killed.

JOHN. (*Perplexed.*) Wendy, surely father didn't use to
sleep in the kennel?

WENDY. (*With misgivings.*) Perhaps we don't remember the old life as well as we thought we did.

JOHN. (*Chilled.*) It is very careless of mother not to be
here when we come back.

(*The PIANO is heard again.*)

WENDY. H'sh! (*She goes to the door and peeps.*) That
is her playing! (*They all have a peep.*)

MICHAEL. Who is that lady?

JOHN. H'sh! It's mother.

MICHAEL. Then are you not really our mother, Wendy?

WENDY. (*With conviction.*) Oh dear, it is quite time to
be back!

JOHN. Let us creep in and put our hands over her eyes.
WENDY. (*More considerate.*) No, let us break it to her
gently.

(*She slips between the sheets of her bed; and the* OTHERS,
*seeing the idea at once, get into their beds. Then
when the MUSIC stops they cover their heads. There
are now three distinct bumps in the beds.* MRS. DAR-
LING *sees the bumps as soon as she comes in, but she
does not believe she sees them.*)

MRS. DARLING. I see them in their beds so often in my
dreams that I seem still to see them when I am awake!
I'll not look again. (*She sits down and turns away her
face from the bumps, though of course they are still reflected
in her mind.*) So often their silver voices call me, my
little children whom I'll see no more.

(*Silver voices is a good one, especially about* JOHN; *but
the heads pop up.*)

WENDY. (*Perhaps rather silvery.*) Mother!
MRS. DARLING. (*Without moving.*) That is Wendy.
JOHN. (*Quite gruff.*) Mother!
MRS. DARLING. Now it is John.
MICHAEL. (*No better than a squeak.*) Mother!
MRS. DARLING. Now Michael. And when they call I
stretch out my arms to them, but they never come, they
never come!

(*This time, however, they come, and there is joy once
more in the* DARLING *household. The little* BOY *who
is crouching at the window sees the joke of the bumps
in the beds, but cannot understand what all the rest
of the fuss is about.*

*The scene changes from the inside of the house to
the outside, and we see* MR. DARLING *romping in at
the door, with the* LOST BOYS *hanging gaily to his
coat-tails. So we may conclude that* WENDY *has told*

*them to wait outside until she explains the situation
to her* MOTHER, *who has then sent* MR. DARLING
*down to tell them that they are adopted. Of course
they could have flown in by the window like a covey
of birds, but they think it better fun to enter by a
door. There is a moment's trouble about* SLIGHTLY,
who somehow gets shut out. Fortunately LIZA *finds
him.*)

LIZA. What is the matter, boy?
SLIGHTLY. They have all got a mother except me.
LIZA. (*Starting back.*) Is your name Slightly?
SLIGHTLY. Yes'm.
LIZA. Then I am your mother.
SLIGHTLY. How do you know?
LIZA. (*The good-natured creature.*) I feel it in my
bones.

(*They go into the house and there is none happier now
than* SLIGHTLY, *unless it be* NANA *as she passes with
the importance of a nurse who will never have another
day off.* WENDY *looks out of the nursery window
and sees a friend below, who is hovering in the
air knocking off tall hats with his feet, The wearers
don't see him. They are too old. You can't see* PETER
*if you are old. They think he is a draught at the
corner.*)

WENDY. Peter!
PETER. (*Looking up casually.*) Hullo, Wendy.

(*She flies down to him, to the horror of her mother, who
rushes to the window.*)

WENDY. (*Making a last attempt.*) You don't feel you
would like to say anything to my parents, Peter, about a
very sweet subject?
PETER. No, Wendy.
WENDY. About me, Peter?

PETER. No. (*He gets out his pipes, which she knows is a very bad sign. She appeals with her arms to* MRS. DARLING, *who is probably thinking that these children will all need to be tied to their beds at night.*)

MRS. DARLING. (*From the window.*) Peter, where are you? Let me adopt you too.

(*She is the cleverest age for a woman, but too old to see* PETER *clearly.*)

PETER. Would you send me to school?
MRS. DARLING. (*Obligingly.*) Yes.
PETER. And then to an office?
MRS. DARLING. I suppose so.
PETER. Soon I should be a man?
MRS. DARLING. Very soon.
PETER. (*Passionately.*) I don't want to go to school and learn solemn things. No one is going to catch me, lady, and make me a man. I want always to be a little boy and to have fun.

(*So perhaps he thinks, but it is only his greatest pretend.*)

MRS. DARLING. (*Shivering every time* WENDY *pursues him in the air.*) Where are you to live, Peter?
PETER. In the house we built for Wendy. The fairies are to put it high up among the tree-tops where they sleep at night.
WENDY. (*Rapturously.*) To think of it!
MRS. DARLING. I thought all the fairies were dead.
WENDY. (*Almost reprovingly.*) No indeed! Their mothers drop the babies into the Never birds' nests, all mixed up with the eggs, and the mauve fairies are boys and the white ones are girls, and there are some colours who don't know what they are. The row the children and the birds make at bath time is positively deafening.
PETER. I throw things at them.
WENDY. You will be rather lonely in the evenings, Peter.

PETER. I shall have Tink.

WENDY. (*Flying up to the window.*) Mother, may I go?

MRS. DARLING. (*Gripping her for ever.*) Certainly not. I have got you home again, and mean to keep you.

WENDY. But he does so need a mother.

MRS. DARLING. So do you, my love.

PETER. Oh, all right.

MRS. DARLING. (*Magnanimously.*) But, Peter, I shall let her go to you once a year for a week to do your spring cleaning.

(WENDY *revels in this, but* PETER, *who has no notion what a spring cleaning is, waves a rather careless thanks.*)

MRS. DARLING. Say good night, Wendy.

WENDY. I couldn't go down just for a minute?

MRS. DARLING. No.

WENDY. Good night, Peter!

PETER. Good night, Wendy!

WENDY. Peter, you won't forget me, will you, before spring-cleaning time comes?

(*There is no answer, for he is already soaring high. For a moment after he is gone we still hear the PIPES. MRS. DARLING closes and bars the windows.*)

We are dreaming now of the Never Land a year later. It is bed-time on the island, and the BLIND goes up to the whispers of the lovely Never MUSIC. The blue haze that makes the wood below magical by day comes up to the tree-tops to sleep, and through it we see numberless nests all lit up, FAIRIES and BIRDS quarrelling for possession, others flying around just for the fun of the thing and perhaps making bets about where the little house will appear tonight. It always comes and snuggles on some tree-top, but you can never be sure which; here it is again, you see JOHN'S hat first as up comes the house so softly that it knocks some gossips of their perch. When it has settled comfortably it LIGHTS UP, and out come PETER *and* WENDY.

WENDY *looks a little older, but* PETER *is just the same. She is cloaked for a journey, and a sad confession must be made about her; she flies so badly now that she has to use a broomstick.*

WENDY. (*Who knows better this time than to be demonstrative at partings.*) Well, good-bye, Peter; and remember not to bite your nails.

PETER. Good-bye, Wendy.

WENDY. I'll tell mother all about the spring cleaning and the house.

PETER. (*Who sometimes forgets that she has been here before.*) You do like the house?

WENDY. Of course it is small. But most people of our size wouldn't have a house at all. (*She should not have mentioned size, for he has already expressed displeasure at her growth. Another thing, one he has scarcely noticed, though it disturbs her, is that she does not see him quite so clearly now as she used to do.*) When you come for me next year, Peter—you will come, won't you?

PETER. Yes. (*Gloating.*) To hear stories about me!

WENDY. It is so queer that the stories you like best should be the ones about yourself.

PETER. (*Touchy.*) Well, then?

WENDY. Fancy your forgetting the lost boys. And even Captain Hook!

PETER. Well, then?

WENDY. I haven't seen Tink this time.

PETER. Who?

WENDY. Oh dear! I suppose it is because you have so many adventures.

PETER. (*Relieved.*) 'Course it is.

WENDY. If another little girl—if one younger than I am— (*She can't go on.*) Oh, Peter, how I wish I could take you up and squdge you! (*He draws back.*) Yes, I know. (*She gets astride her broomstick.*) Home! (*It carries her from him over the tree-tops.*)

(*In a sort of way he understands what she means by "Yes, I know," but in most sorts of ways he doesn't. It has something to do with the riddle of his being. If he could get the hang of the thing his cry might become "To live would be an awfully big adventure!" but he can never quite get the hang of it, and so no one is as gay as he. With rapturous face he produces his pipes, and the Never* BIRDS *and the* FAIRIES *gather closer till the roof of the little house is so thick with his admirers that some of them fall down the chimney. He plays on and on till we wake up.*)

The End

PRINTED AND BOUND IN GREAT BRITAIN FOR
HODDER AND STOUGHTON LIMITED, ST. PAUL'S
HOUSE, WARWICK LANE, LONDON, E.C.4
BY C. TINLING AND CO. LIMITED, LIVERPOOL,
LONDON AND PRESCOT